STOOL WIVES

PLOVER NIVOLA SERIES
A LIBRARY OF POST-1950's FICTION

On the Window Licks the Night by John Mitchell
Channel Zero by Michael Krekorian
Stool Wives by William F. Van Wert

About the Cover
"This stool may refer to the ruler's dependence on the sobriety and equilibrium of the women who helped to maintain his hegemony."

—*African Art: From Crocodiles to Convertibles in the Collection of the Seattle Art Museum*
by Pamela McClusky

Stool Wives

A Fiction of Africa
by

William F. Van Wert

Plover Press
Kaneohe, Hawaii
1996

Printed and bound in the United States of America

Cover art: Kihona (stool) and Kente Cloth: Aberewa Bene
(detail). "The Seattle Art Museum." Gift of Katherine White
and the Boeing Company. Photo Credit: Paul Macapia.

Library of Congress Cataloging-in-Publication Data

Van Wert, William F.
    Stool wives : a fiction of Africa / by William F. Van Wert.
       p.   cm. — (Plover nivola series)
    ISBN 0-917635-20-5 (hard : alk. paper)
    1. Ibo (African people)—Kings and rulers—Fiction.
  2. Young men—Nigeria—Fiction.   3. Africa—Fiction.
I. Title. II. Series.
PS3572.A4228 S76   1996
813'.54—dc20   95-50641
                                              CIP

Distributed by
Academy Chicago Publishers
363 West Erie Street
Chicago, IL 60610

For David

For My Sons

Ian is not on Sinai
O David, diva do. Evade Dave.
Poor Dan is in a droop.

"You can't just leave a body on the highway," she said. "It's immoral."

It was one instance in which I did not distrust the word, because she meant something quite specific. She meant that if a body is left alone for even a few minutes on the desert, the coyotes close in and eat the flesh. Whether or not a corpse is torn apart by coyotes may seem only a sentimental consideration, but of course it is more: one of the promises we make to one another is that we will try to retrieve our casualties, try not to abandon our dead to the coyotes.

—Joan Didion, *On Morality*

STOOL WIVES

I

As was the custom in the Ibo tribes of northeastern Nigeria, the rural kings were always picked by height and height alone. He would be king who towered over all others in the tribe. When another proclaimed that he was taller than the king, he could challenge his sovereign, in which case the challenger was measured at the sacred baobab tree, in view of the whole tribe. If indeed he was taller, he was made king and there was great rejoicing and feasting for days and days. But if he merely tied the king or was in fact shorter than the king, then the challenger was punished and could never again challenge his king. In this case there was still great feasting and rejoicing, for the king was reaffirmed and young boys went through a period of renewed respect for their elders.

In olden days, when the baobab tree was still alive and bore fruit, the challenger was sometimes

1

beheaded, and his head was hung from the highest branch, so that his spirit would soar and be tall, and birds of prey came to sing the praises of the victorious king. In more recent times the practice of beheading had been discontinued, except in the most extreme cases (either the challenger had bragged too much or was not contrite enough at losing or the king was especially ornery and spiteful or perhaps he was getting old and shrinking just a tad). The long years of exposure to British colonial rule and excessive contact with Christian missionaries had taken their toll on the tribes and made them more merciful, so that failed challengers no longer feared becoming food for crows and eagles, but had instead to endure a lifetime of being the butt of many cruel taunts, not the least of which was the following, from cackling old women and brazen children: "Your head is in the trees." Or: "Tall boy, did you eat crow or did the crow eat you?" In this way the Ibo tribes carried out in words what they no longer did in deeds. For them, as for the Edo tribes, words and deeds were approximately the same thing, after all was said and done.

Over the long hall of time there were not so many challengers, even with softer, more seductive punishments, for in the subsistence farming communities most men bent their backs to the land, to plough and furrow, hammer and rut, machete and fertilize. To worry about would-be things like kingship was considered both honorable and aberrant, and the stool wives were forever being blamed for implanting such ambitions in their young sons.

Yet in the tribe of Joseph Odoki there was a young man named Kimbene who would not give up the dream. At seventeen he was six feet and seven inches, with the prospect of still growing, and he schemed with his short friend Ngugi.

"I would be king," Kimbene said, "and that is all, if design govern in a thing so tall."

"You speak well," Ngugi said, "for a tall boy."

"I speak in trance when I want a thing so bad, and trance is dance and dance is rhyme and rhyme is time . . ."

"Enough of it, mahn. Save such speeches for the throne."

"You are so wise, Ngugi. Why have you stood by me these many years?"

"Because you did not spit on me for being short or kick me or make me carry your water pail."

"And?"

"And because you are a tall boy with lofty dreams."

"And?"

"And because you are malleable."

"Maybe I am asking the wrong question," Kimbene said.

"Then ask the right question."

"What did you want to be when you grew up, Ngugi, mahn?"

"William Shakespeare."

"Ha. You are not so wise."

"I have answered your question. If you ask the right question, you will find me wise."

"You speak in riddles. Me, mahn, all I ever wanted to be was king."

"So now you can ask the right question."

"Well, then, what is it in me you admire most?"

"The will to power."

These and many other dialogues ensued. The two boys grew to be men. They bonded as men. They drank from the same gourd, shared the same fire, told the same stories and measured themselves by the same ox-breadth. And all the while Ngugi was training Kimbene for the day he would be king, the salad days of sovereignty.

"You are the beast that makes promises," Ngugi said.

"Have you been smoking hemp again?"

"Nay, mahn."

"The Sahara comes South by a foot every day. I will rule over click beetles in dry sand at the rate I am going."

"No, for I have thought of a way."

"Then say."

"It's in a play."

"How many times have I told you that reading is dangerous for grown men? I suppose the play is by William Shakespeare?"

"And what of it?"

"Wole Soyinka is our William Shakespeare. You should be reading black wordsmiths. For pride."

"Perhaps you are not as malleable as I thought, Kimbene."

4

"I have offended your feathers. Tell me, mahn, about the play."

"It is *Dick the Third*. In the Third Dick I have found a way, but you must trust me."

"Yes, but am I tall enough? Joe Odoki does not have so many stool wives for nothing. Whenever he appears in public, he is always sitting, so there is no way to measure him. And I don't want to lose."

"Measure for measure, I have measured him."

"How can this be? He does not permit of anyone up close."

"I have measured his throne when he was not in it. From the ground to the seat. This gives me the lower body. For the upper body I have measured the shadow he cast at the last feasting. The shadow makes approximately two of the thing that throws the shadow. By my computations he is six feet and six, maybe six feet and seven, but not more."

"I cannot trust to your computations, Ngugi."

"Then will you trust to more devious means? I have bribed his driver, who got it from one of the stool wives who looked when Joe Odoki was sleeping and saw his driver's license, which says he is six and seven."

"Then I can only tie. I must wait until I have grown another inch."

"Did Hakeem Olajuwon wait to grow another inch before going to America, their space basketball, to Houston Rockets, who pay him millions of dollars, more money than Live Aid?"

"Yes, but he was over seven in feet tallness. He

could have been king of our tribe, no sweating. And yet he went to play bounce-the-ball and slam-dunking, all this repetition of putting roundness where there is absence. I have heard he was awkward at soccer, which we value far more."

"But the Americans will not pay millions for soccer. They pay for his tallness to play out their ballness, so that they can sit like Joe Odoki with their stool wives and remain idle. They have no kings, and so they hero whom they can own. Have you not pondered the strange sameness between idle and idol, these English words that tell us what we want to know of history, politics and philosophy?"

"No, I never one time pondered it."

"Then answer me this question. Would you rather be Hakeem Olajuwon in Houston's high-toned old Christian housing or would you rather be rural king?"

"I would rather be rural king."

"This is not the smart answer, but it is the right answer for our intensive purposes."

"Yes, but how does it make me taller than Joe Odoki?"

"By ruse and dupery."

"This is a main street in Paris, no?"

"My dear Kimbene, I merely speak Shakespearean."

"Speak to me plain, then."

"By furtive complicity, then."

"This is surely better, I jest."

"You must begin to act Best Western."

"This is not the way to win the hearts of liberated peoples. They will see through me as bamboo."

"There will be time and plenty later, when you are rural king, for naturalizing all your alienated subjects."

"By feasting."

"Yes. Spectacles are one way."

"By driving a plainer car than Joe Odoki. Bigger, but plainer."

"This too."

"By stool wives. I can have my pick."

"As many as Lot had salt to lick his wounds."

And so it came to pass. The time for dialoguing deeds was done. The time for doing deeds had come. Kimbene issued a formal challenge to Joe Odoki. Under the tutelage of Ngugi, Kimbene had already begun to wear western clothes and hang about in heavy-scented ways. And thus he went unnoticed when he began to wear the elevator shoes Ngugi bought on a secret trip to Lagos. Kimbene could not take three steps in the new shoes without falling, so Ngugi passed around the tribe a story that Kimbene had injured his leg, which explained the shepherd's staff he used when he walked.

When the appointed day came, both Joe Odoki and Kimbene stood up against the baobab tree, and at the top of each head, men with machetes made marks in the tree. The women began a cadence of cricket sounds and bird-chirps, which built to a crescendo and broke into loud whelping and wailing when it was announced that the mark of Kimbene was the taller of the two.

Looking at Kimbene's quaint western dress, his bulky shoes and shepherd's staff, Joe Odoki passed the crown to his adversary with a prophecy.

"I fear the dark days are upon us," he said.

"Praise our blackness," Ngugi screamed, turning Odoki's slander into a slogan that echoed around the tribe.

Kimbene had been well-rehearsed and he was gracious in victory.

"And praise to you, Odoki mahn, for it is right and just and praise the past we must. You have been a kindly king, and so there will be no talking of beheadings. You are free to keep your stool wives and take your English Ford to another tribe, to retire gracefully and count your grandchildren."

And so Joe Odoki moved on, shunned by the tribe, with beads and gourds and all manner of gift-giving, enough to fill the Ford, but his name remained, to be memorized by all the children as part of the litany of all things lost.

II

It was a time of terrible feasting. Just as in Africa there is always a time of terrible famine, so too there is occasionally terrible feasting, and such was the case at the coronation of Kimbene as rural king. His realm and ruraldom did not extend beyond the boundaries of his physical vision, occupying a corner of northeastern Nigeria so small and insignificant that it had no name. Five miles away, the neighboring tribes were unaware of a change in kings, but this fact cut no ice with young Kimbene. Swelled by his superior height and the freshness of his mandate, Kimbene was determined not to be outdone by his predecessors, and so he proclaimed an orgy of feasting. From wild boar to water buffalo to brood mare, every beast of burden was sacrificed. Even the plough-oxen were unfettered and slaughtered at the spit. There were rice cakes and ground corn, mango and pineapple, palm wine and warm beer for everyone. People passed out and had to be carried away. Others went into trance while dancing and stayed possessed for weeks. The children smoked hemp and listened to stories of magical boasting, of tricking and fooling, a philosophy of cathexis and warrior prowess. Stories of mighty valor mixed with stories of accidental excreta, and both met with rousing rounds of whooping, hollering, knee-slapping and approving. It was not within the rights of subjects to object to feasting, even when the sugar ripened and died uncut in the canebrakes and the rice turned to parched rabbit pellets in the paddies. The tribe had no consciousness of its own vulnerability during feasting, whose ritualized excesses were thought to be safeguards against enemy incursions, famine and disease. Merriment by decree.

There was wrestling and fist-fighting in the morning, for those young boys who were strong enough and sober enough to make an impression. There was dozing, napping, trance-dreams and sleep-walking in the afternoons, when the sun was too hot to allow little else; and when darkness came, then came the massive campfire, the drinking and dancing, the stories and boasting, the sexual thrust and parry. The day's routine came to be known as fisting, then fasting, then feasting, and Kimbene was the ideal rural king: he ate and sucked grease from his fingers; he danced in public and spoke in dialect; he drove an ordinary car, a Volvo, in wagon-train circles around the campfire; he boasted and toasted the whole tribe.

In his first week as rural king he took three stool wives, whose names were Stella, Della and Naomi, even though the last of these, the mysterious Naomi, was a notorious man-hater and had vowed to remain a virgin her entire life. These three sat stool behind Kimbene, their king. They danced when he danced, they laughed when he laughed, and they went off with him, singly or in pairs, when that was his bidding. Within the first two months of feasting, Stella and Della came down with spells, and by their off-key singing and irritability it was conveyed to the king and his tribe that both were pregnant. Without pausing for nature to decide the gender of his issue, Kimbene, himself convulsed with fertility—for in Africa men swell along with their women—proclaimed that the offspring would be sons and that they would be called Mike and Moustafa, in that order. Stella and Della were both leeched, to the delight of everyone, and only Naomi sat still on her stool like a dream deferred.

It was the responsibility of the rural king to make a toast before each boast at the evening feasting around the enormous campfire. Thus Kimbene said: "Brothers, may all your sisters give you blisters, and, sisters, may all your brothers make you mothers." Before saying: "The eagle looks up to me." And when one of the sober ones reminded him that he had mixed up the order from time to time, he began again, for he was not short on either toasts or boasts.

"That we may get what we want, need and deserve . . . in that order," he toasted.

"Long after the wood of their stools has rotted, my wives may have a place to sit as long as I have a face," he boasted.

Nothing was censured or abridged, as it is in more urbanized cultures of the West.

Even the anal was accepted as a sign of intimacy, and the whole tribe cheered when Kimbene defecated onto the fire without receiving any flesh burns. Others tried to replicate this feat and were sorely awakened from their delusional dreams of representation.

The rural king was also responsible for the musical accompaniment to feasting. Kimbene chose a variety of musical delights for his subjects: some Otis Redding, some Italian opera, some Gregorian chant. Nothing was censured or abridged, and people danced to whatever music with the same pulse and passion.

One day a man tried to put a bomb in the campfire, but it was an old British bomb, with no potency left, and the man was found out, rather than blowing up with his wishes. At first, Kimbene threatened to behead the man, but the feasting was still going strong and the mood was wrong. Then he threatened bondage, but there were objections to this recourse as well. So, he forgave the man and ordered the man to go beat his fetish. This show of mercy was not lost on the king's subjects, who made him grow even taller with their approval.

An ambassador from the regional king arrived unexpectedly. In the hierarchy of ruling kings at that time, there were many rural kings and above them a few regional kings. This ambassador came from the regional king, whose name was Achebe, but whose face no one in the tribe had ever seen. The regional king may not walk among his people, does not permit of any touching by his people, and no longer speaks the dialects of his subjects, but rather speaks through a linguist. And so it was that Sosa, the personal linguist of Achebe, was in the entourage of the ambassador, and he gave his message to Kimbene.

"He in whom I am well pleased, be."

This message was taken to be a miracle by all the people of the tribe, but Kimbene wondered privately at the stern face of Sosa, the arcane inversion of the language, which emphasized the stilts of translation over the shoes of truth.

"Abraham Lincoln looks up to you," the ambassador said, bestowing beads and fetishes all around.

After the royal guests had departed, Kimbene made many toasts and boasts at the evening's feasting, got thoroughly drunk and tried to seduce the sedentary Naomi off her stool. Failing in this, he tried to fool her off her stool, with stories of red ants and plague. Failing in this, he took her by force to his tent, where the tribal crones and gossips were rumored to overhear the thumping and whacking of a fetish.

The next morning Kimbene crawled out of his tent with bees in his brain and a black eye. Immediately, he proclaimed that all the warriors of his tribe should likewise blacken one of their eyes,

13

which they did post-haste with pitch and tar and self-inflicted wounds. The smarter ones had recourse to masking and simulacra. Those less gifted took the more literal path.

The story of the eye brought Kimbene to break from feasting, so that he might walk among his people, especially the indigent, the old, the blind, the lepered, the slim, all those who lived off the mercy of the tribe. Kimbene felt neither pity nor indignation at the sight of so many who could not help themselves. But, in so far as he was their king and they reflected upon the image of his kingship, he mocked them. He put his hands in his pockets and acted idly for the indigent. He stooped over and shuffled for the elderly. He rolled his eyes for the blind, until only the whites were visible. And he constricted his ribcage and smeared his face with grease and flour for the lepers, until he looked as deformed as they. These acts of mimesis were not lost on them. To a man they praised the pliability of their rural king.

And when it was brought to his attention that so much feasting had severely depleted his financial resources, Kimbene did not discontinue the feasting. Instead he sent his pregnant wives, Stella and Della, to mingle among the populace and steal as much money as they could. They were more or less practiced in the art of purloin, which is to say that after a time the people were wise to them. They made no protest. They simply hid their money and came to the campfire without a coin of the realm. Now it was Kimbene's turn, not to protest, but

rather to mock them with games of bingo, monopoly, craps and the like, for which his subjects were
ill-prepared to play. And so they began to bring
their money again. In this way not a word was said
and much was accomplished.

Redundancy is often more a matter of coherence
and intensity than of repetition. Thus it was that
Kimbene thought of repeated feasting as alchemists of old thought of transforming metals: that
is, as a way of ironizing irony. He had no firm
agenda for being rural king, except to stand taller
than the rest of his tribe and have incredible sex
with stool wives. He had in mind to educate his
tribe as he, himself, got educated, so that eventu-
ally he planned to make speeches on various problems of rural, regional and national interest: the ar-
tichoke of apartheid in the south; the inflation of
the United Nations by third-world countries, most
of which were springing up in Africa; map-reading
for the masses; the persecution of the Jews; the metaphor of basketball replacing that of slavery in the
black consciousness; the end of safaris in a post-
colonial consciousness; the importance of Franco
on the ego-formation of Idi Amin; the loss of hamlet, town and traditional dressing gown to the cities. He had in mind to speak of all these things
when he had physically found the voice to do so,
for it was strongly believed at that time that voice
played hide-and-seek with knowledge. Anyone
could come by knowledge, but not everyone can
find a voice. In fact, the purpose of telling tall tales
in African cultures is to stumble onto a true voice.

And Kimbene realized that his youth still begged for what his height already knew. And so he kept on feasting.

In all this time he still had not coaxed Naomi into becoming his concubine, and he was beginning to despair, for divorce, like monogamy, was still thought of as a western custom, a thing of decadence, a taint, a blot. But then it was suggested to him that her virginity only served to emphasize the fertility of Stella and Della, and comparative emphasis was often more compelling than empirical truths. Kimbene was convinced by this argument, and he quelled his lust for the unattainable by treating Naomi as though she were his dowry sow and by thinking of her in terms of Hegelian hope: that is, at the end of history her spirit would be his.

All rural kingships go through a communist phase before they attain the full materiality of vampirism, or capitalism, and so it was that someone produced an argument of such Zen-Bataille proportions that Kimbene was persuaded to listen. The argument went that the true king should give all of his wealth to the least of his subjects. This he did. In full view of the entire tribe he emptied his coffers and gave all his material wealth to the leper Leopold, who was so far beyond abrasions that he could not be helped. But then Kimbene asked Leopold to extend the arrangement logically, which meant that Leopold should give all his newfound wealth to him who had none, who was, of course, the smiling Kimbene. But, lest the tribe should think him too bold and bald-faced a beggar, Kimbene went one step further. He africanized the argument. He reasoned thus: what is treasured above all else in my tribe? The answer? Fertility. So, Kimbene dressed himself up with a pillow encased inside his dashiki, that he might appear pregnant, knowing full well that to appear is to forget, to seem is already to stand halfway in dream. By this ploy he played upon the sympathies of his subjects. He sat very close to Naomi with the pillow bulging at his midriff, for he knew that her name had become synonymous with that-which-does-not-occur, and he also knew there is nothing more poignant to African eyes than a man who deludes himself by thinking he is with child. The shame-faced leper Leopold could not turn a deaf ear to all the wailing women around him, and so he gave all the wealth back to Kimbene.

In this way Kimbene resumed his rural kingship, having doubled both his pleasure and his own entendre.

III

It was during the time of terrible feasting that the rural king Kimbene came under the influence, some called it the spell, of Perry Lumumba, whose eccentricity was that he spoke only in palindromes. Even his brothers, all named by Perry instead of his parents, were palindromic, but also political, as is often the case with language. People referred to them as Perry Lumumba and his younger brothers, as though there were only two entities, when in fact the brothers were three: Idi, Lon Nol and Bob, respectively, all named for political figures.

How Kimbene came under the influence of Perry Lumumba was a simple and inarticulate thing. Perry, who barely stood six feet tall, represented no rivalry in height for Kimbene, and so he was allowed to come to the evening campfire with his gift for the new rural king. The gift was a string of coral beads, highly valued, with one kola nut in the middle or at either end of the string, depending upon how one held it. Now the kola nut was code, symbolic of offering a bribe, but in this case an empty bribe, since it was surrounded by the highly valued coral beads. Kimbene surveyed the string of beads for an unconscionably long time, although time has no measure or value in terms of length among the Ibo, and then he looked into the strange eyes of the donor, one brown, the other blue, and finally he broke into a laughing fit. The tribe laughed nervously with its king, for people young and old, and especially the elders, thought a beheading was at hand, to mix a metaphor.

They were wrong. Kimbene ordered a stool next to his stool wives, upon which Perry was bade to put his bones. This he did, with a bouncy insouciance and a certain pelvic rhythm which surprised Kimbene. The latter laughed again.

"You shall be my personal fool, Perrymahn."

But Perry shook his head no.

"Fool aloof," he said.

"Well, you may be aloof, but you're still my fool. As long as laughter is so freely given, what is mine is yours."

Perry reacted by looking lasciviously at the stool wives.

"Within reason, Perrymahn," Kimbene cautioned, for the sharing of stool wives was much joked about but strictly taboo.

"I have taken three stool wives," Kimbene continued. "But I don't know if I should take more or not. What, pray you tell, is the right number of stool wives?"

"Never odd or even," Perry said, and everyone cheered his wit and sagacity.

But over the long hall of time, the corridor of temporality, the aisle of the actual unfolding, Perry Lumumba was not uniformly witty or sagacious. He could flare like a brown bull, his wide nostrils widening, until one might say gyre, instead of nose. He could show pique and tic, and the only safeguard against his spontaneity was that his speech was palindromic, his utterance was a train going backwards and forwards, a caboose at both ends. Kimbene could trust in what he, himself, could never possess: a sense of history that was neither linear nor circular, a sense of politics that imploded upon itself, like the kola nut on a string of coral beads. The truly eccentric can only be dangerous if one assumes an eventual identity crisis, that one must become eccentric like the eccentric or that the eccentric must be rendered normal. Kimbene assumed neither of these collisions. In his search for an authentic African voice, he was grateful that Perry fulfilled a need for a voice that Kimbene could never make his, and so didn't have to. The more voices he could gather to his chorus, the fewer he would have to master personally for his own authentic voice.

This did not mean that he had gathered a yesmahn to his bosom. He soon discovered how difficult Perry could be. He soon found out that the same eccentric he by turns admired he by turns had to tolerate, put up or shut up with, wish secretly to behead, and that the same humor that tickles also comes from a cutting edge.

He ordered Perry to go for a spin with him in the royal Volvo around the evening campfire, but Perry refused and stayed seated on his stool next to Stella and Della. Kimbene had never expected to see a royal order refused so soon or so openly in his rural kingship. Apparently, the Volvo wasn't ordinary enough, as vehicles go, so Kimbene asked what kind of car Perrymahn would ride around in.

"A Toyota," he said, and the whole tribe responded with a collective "of course" by shrugging their shoulders and nodding their heads.

Once the unexpected answer came and there was such a thing as retrospect, the answer was then not only expected but inevitable.

And when Kimbene defecated on the flames, Perry responded by spitting at the fire. His unsavory spittle, for there was a raucous throat-clearing and a certain dense phlegm associated with his spit, unsettled the elders and incensed one Brother Jero, a fat and most pompous man who spoke with an Oxford English and headed the dreaded Board of Interviews.

"Brother Perry," Brother Jero said, making a point of hollowly clearing his own throat, "don't expect to rate if you expectorate."

"Yes, Perrymahn," Kimbene said, himself a bit put off because his defecation had been upstaged, "why do you do this?"

"Spit tips," Perry said, the laconic merging with the prophetic.

"He says," Kimbene said, translating for the tribe, "that his spitball is a prerequisite to good advice, for which we are grateful."

Indeed, it was Perry Lumumba who tipped off his king to the terrorism of the British bomb that never went off. Perry spit into the fire, leaned over to Kimbene and whispered in the tall king's ear.

"Party boobytrap," he whispered.

Perry could do no wrong after that. His loyalty to the king was secure, a sailor's knot, a foregone conclusion. It never surfaced that the would-be assassin, a doltish man named Loki, was in the employ of Lon Nol Lumumba, himself a hothead anarchist, who didn't know the difference between a church and Churchill, a skate and a cheapskate, a paradox and two doctors, a cleaving from a cleaving.

And when Kimbene decided against beheading Loki and was still contemplating some form of indentured servitude, Perry Lumumba led the cry for clemency.

"Egad," he said, "no bondage."

But he was not so lenient when it came to campfire music. In fact, he was downright implacable. Kimbene had just settled upon Otis Redding singing "Sitting on the Dock of the Bay," when Perrymahn spat into the flames.

"Sit on a potato pan, Otis," he grumbled.

So, Kimbene switched to opera.

"Paganini—din in a gap," Perry snorted.

Gregorian chant won the day, Kimbene suspected, not because Perry was soothed by its papal infallibility, but rather because Perry was unable to find a palindrome to refute it. This is often the case with Catholic things, which go unrefuted by the less palindromic too.

Perry proved to be something of a prude about sex as well. When Kimbene went about whacking Stella or Della during the noon hour, at which time the rest of his tribe was resting, the ever-vigilant Perry flared a warning with his nostrils.

"Sex at noon taxes," he warned.

And when Kimbene took the nihilistic Naomi to his tent by force one night and emerged the next morning with a hangover and the heavy lid of a black eye, Perry was there on all fours, playing the fool.

"Naomi, did I moan?" he screeched in falsetto.

"Shut up, Perrymahn."

"Sore eye, Eros?"

"Shut up, Perrymahn."

"Senile felines."

"That's my wife you're talking about, fool."

"Solo gigolos."

"Do you wish to be a eunuch?"

At that, Perry succumbed to silence, having scored the pride of his monarch severely.

The story of the eye, as is well known, gave way to a rupture, a break from fasting, when Kimbene went walking among his people, especially the indigent, the old, the blind, the lepered, the slim, all those who lived off the mercy of the tribe. Perry cheered when Kimbene mocked them, making them into caricature from tragedy, but at the sight of Leopold, the leper, Perry could not contain his disgust, and he spat upon Leopold, who was both censured and abridged with scabs and sores, both closed and open, the stuck smegma of society.

"Lepers repel," Perry said, pointing to Leopold. "Bird rib."

What Perry gave away in compassion, he quickly took back in cruelty, which was both pert and earnest, if anything.

Kimbene felt neither pity nor indignation at the sight of so many who could not help themselves. He simply mocked them and took mental note, knowing full well he would have reason to return to them.

And when it was brought to his attention that so much feasting had severely depleted his financial resources, Kimbene did not discontinue the feasting. Instead he sent his pregnant wives, Stella and Della, to mingle among the populace and steal as much money as they could.

When the stool wives came back empty-handed, Perry tattled on them.

"Stella won no wallets," he whispered in the tall king's ear.

Kimbene, who was busy making toasts and boasts, was grateful for this petty surveillance.

"Then beat her with my fetish," Kimbene whispered back, "but not around the belly."

Now it was Kimbene's turn, not to protest, but rather to mock his people with games of bingo, monopoly, craps and the like, for which his subjects were ill-prepared to play. And so they began to bring their money again. In this way not a word was said and much was accomplished.

Redundancy is often more a matter of coherence and intensity than of repetition. Thus it was that Kimbene thought of repeated feasting as alchemists of old thought of transforming metals: that is, as a way of ironizing irony. He had no firm agenda for being rural king, except to stand taller than the rest of his tribe and have incredible sex with stool wives.

And when it was suggested that the true king should give all of his wealth to the least of his subjects, Kimbene did so. He summoned Leopold, the leper, to the evening feasting. But then Kimbene asked Leopold to extend the arrangement logically, which meant that Leopold should give all his newfound wealth to him who had none, who was, of course, the smiling Kimbene. Leopold was not wont to do this, for lepers can be notoriously cunning and greedy creatures, but Perry Lumumba spat on him and whispered in his claymation ear.

"Live evil . . . die trap aparteid."

Leopold may have been incurably diseased, but he was not stupid. He understood the implied threat behind Perry's words, and to the chorus of wailing women, who were bereaved that Kimbene should look so false-pregnant with a pillow encased in his dashiki, Leopold returned the wealth to its rightful owner, his rural king.

Perry thought his threat should have been sufficient and was a bit peeved that Kimbene had deemed it necessary to introduce hysteria by way of the surreptitious pillow. When the rest of the tribe had returned to toasting, boasting, telling tall tales, standing erect and pissing into the fire, Perry expressed his disdain in a private way to his king.

"Pillow? AWOL lip."

In this way Perry let Kimbene know that desire depended upon an absence, an AWOL lip, a deferral over time. That Perry knew this much seemed a dangerous thing to Kimbene, who resolved to espy his fool more closely, him and his younger brothers Idi, Lon Nol and Bob.

IV

Was it simply a case of coronation feasting going on too long? Or was there some secret principle of eternal return at work, given that order is a kind of compulsion to repeat? Nobody knew. The only truth of which anyone could be certain in the nameless Ibo tribe of that time was that the same space cannot have two different contents. And so it was that Ngugi, the stub-counsellor who begat a king, had been absent, himself deferred nicely over time, but not idle.

He found Kimbene one morning outside the royal tent, prone, the whole of him splayed in drunken stupor, his face in a puddle of palm wine. Ngugi was saddened at this sight. He helped his king and boyhood friend to an erect state, which was no small feat, on account of his squatness and Kimbene's drunkenness.

"Ngugimahn, long time no see. Would you like some warm beer?"

"Regal lager," Perry Lumumba said from his crouch nearby, his whole body contorted to a hunch, a guess, a supposition.

Ngugi declined. The stench of stale breath after beer gagged him.

"You know Perry," Kimbene said. "I have made him my favorite. But I must warn you, he doesn't much care for the classics, and that would include your Shakespeare."

"Avon bard? Drab nova," Perry said, spitting for emphasis.

"Get thee hence, thou cream-faced loon," Ngugi said to Perry.

"You have to admit his star has risen and shines dimly," Kimbene said in defense of Perry, but, seeing that Ngugi was near boiling point with rage, he demurred.

"Take five, Perrymahn. A king has need of more than a fool to rule."

Perry left with some reluctance. Then the two old friends spoke.

"I have missed you at the feasting, Ngugi."

"I have not been idle."

"So? Tell me what keeps you away from your king."

"My spies followed Joe Odoki. He went straight-away to the regional king to complain of foul play."

"Achebe?"

"Himself. So, I took precautions. Look to the East. What do you see?"

"Is this mirage?" Kimbene asked.

The sacred baobab tree, long dead but still revered, was gone. In its stead was a shed, a lean-to, with a cross on top.

"No. I have dispatched the baobab to a zoo in America for dollars in the thousands. They say the zebra will not accept any other habitat than a baobab."

"But why a church instead?"

"The bloody missionaries. They may come to our corner of the country, but they will see the cross, think we are saved believers and move on. I have killed two crow with one throw."

"You are indeed the wise one. But what about the other evidence? What about my elevator shoes?"

"I sent them to Ethiopia, where some Selassie-mahn may make good use of them."

"Did you get dollars for them?"

"No. They sent back a pillow. They say it is a sovereign pillow and has magical powers. And you, Kimbene, have you done nothing but toast and boast?"

"I have been waterworking my kingship, as you instructed, just like Hexley says to do."

"Huxley."

"No matter then. This tribe has never had more circuses."

"And less bread."

"I have made two babies in the bowels of my stool wives."

31

"They will cancel out the two who have starved to death. The sugar cane sours. The rice crop is ruined. There is more to kingship than fisting and fasting and feasting."

"Then you must teach me how to rule, my dear Ngugimahn, without censure or abridgment."

This Ngugi tried to do. But he could not always predict the actions of his king. He could only put them into a broader context. And so when Kimbene defecated upon the fire, Ngugi spoke quietly to the crowd about powerful deflections, of an impulse no longer inhibited in its aim, and he encouraged the young warriors of the tribe to put out the fire by micturating, which term they didn't understand, but which instinct they possessed in great abundance.

And when the personal linguist of the regional king had spoken to Kimbene, Ngugi personally escorted the linguist away from the feasting, with gifts of many coral beads and outrageous praise for the invisible Achebe.

Ngugi was not especially taken with any of the stool wives of Kimbene, but when Naomi blackened the eye of Kimbene, Ngugi saw his chance to make a rupture with feasting.

"You must walk among your people, Kimbene."

"Why? Because they are poor?"

"No. Because they are resentful."

"Oh that. I envy them."

And when Kimbene mocked his subjects with pratfalls and mimesis, Ngugi could only wince and shake his head in wonder. The leper Leopold was a sacred thing within the tribe because he was so made-over and misshapen, and Ngugi feared that Kimbene might be destooled by the regional king if he made a mockery of someone who had been so lampooned by good fortune, but once again Kimbene surprised him. He told Leopold some off-color Biafran jokes which made Leopold laugh, which laughter caused several scabs to burst from which pus ran freely as a gazelle. Thus, sadism, the other side of happy laughter, was brought into being, and no one was the wiser.

Redundancy is often more a matter of coherence and intensity than of repetition. Thus it was that Kimbene thought of repeated . . . etc. And suddenly Kimbene was troubled and sought counsel from his friend Ngugi.

"Do you think, Ngugimahn, that there is an arbitrariness to the way each day eats up the preceding day or do you think sometimes time stutters and we are stuck in circumstances we have lived before but are unable to prevent?"

"This is either the predestination question or the reincarnation question. At this stage in your development, you are ready for neither."

"But there are so many topics I want to speak to, and instead I am rooted in circumstance. A man tries to bomb me, I defecate on the ritual flames, I get a black eye from my stool wife, I . . ."

"You cannot help it, Kimbene. This is what becoming Best Western means."

"Stay with me yet awhile, for I am troubled."

"I will stay with you forever, Kimbene friend."

And so it went. It was Ngugi who suggested to Kimbene that the virginity of Naomi only served to emphasize the fertility of Stella and Della, and that comparative emphasis was often more compelling than empirical truths. It was Ngugi who suggested that Kimbene should give all of his wealth to the least of his subjects, even though Lon Nol Lumumba went around acting empty-handed and competed with Leopold the leper for that dubious distinction. And it was Ngugi who provided the miracle midriff, by suggesting that Kimbene stuff the magical Ethiopian pillow into his dashiki.

And when Kimbene at last tired of fires, of toasting and boasting, it was Ngugi who read to him at bedtime on nights when Naomi said she slept with the dead and would not go near him. In this way that rare commodity—friendship—saved the sanity of the young rural king.

V

There were many interdictions and superstitions among the Ibo, but two precepts held primacy over all others, and those were the following: that women controlled the fire and that writing was in its origin the voice of an absent person. We shall see how these two came to be related.

The Prometheus myth was known to the people of Kimbene's tribe, but it was disavowed as Best Western propaganda. The conventional wisdom went something like this: men controlled the earth, the water and air, the three known elements of prehistoric times. Women invented fire, to attract their men back home from the hunt, to make sex more possible on cold days, and to distract themselves on days when their men were away. Women learned to cook with fire as a self-defense mechanism, because men who were bad hunters would come home from the hunt resentful and pride-pocked, and they would want to eat their women and children. Women learned how to start the fire and keep the fire. It fell to men to react to the fire in a symptomatic way, the way they had learned to react to women sexually. The purpose of fire for men was to piss it out. This was not possible on all fours. So man stood up, became the *homo erectus* that we know today, so that he could take better aim at the fire. It cost him a great deal of rear-entry advantage on women, but it taught him the twin purposes of the penis: to extinguish women and fires.

As to writing, a similar historical trajectory can be traced. It makes good sense that writing was in its origins the voice of an absent person. More obviously, in presence, the opposite of absence, speech takes precedence over writing, to the extent that writing is banished when a tribe is in full attendance. But writing was created by women as well. When prehistoric men went off to hunt or forage, women were left alone in caves. This was fine as long as they had food and kept the fires burning. But if the men stayed gone too long or if the fire went out, the women were forced to move, and they left messages scrawled in stone on the cave walls. Such messages were relatively simple and to the point. They said: "Fire went out" or "Lion ate Ajax and we moved on."

To this day, writing is equated with absence for the Ibo, and absence is the worst fear of all, even exceeding fears of famine, war, disease or death. Presence is the prerequisite for all life. Absence is the abyss. Speech is prepared for and perfected at an early age. Writing is deferred, distrusted as a form of alienation.

The constants in both cases are women and absence.

The story of Moses and Aaron was known to Kimbene and the people of his tribe from the many missionaries who came to them during the days of British rule. But their interpretation of the story ran counter to the Christian version. They believed that punishment preceded the law, that the golden calf worship and many hedonisms were rampant during Moses' absence, so that his return was not enough. He had to come back with the tablets. And when he returned from the burning bush, he came with writing, not direct speech. Worse, he came back lisping, so that his brother Aaron, who had been silent and ruling with a rod up to that point, had to become the interpreter, the speaker, the personal linguist of his regional king. This was how Kimbene and his tribe kept the story, once it was transmitted to them. They saw Moses as a womanly figure. An Ibo warrior would have pissed out the fire of the burning bush and come down the mountain without any tablets, his speech intact. He would have told tall tales about his trip, and that would have been that.

Similarly, they did not believe in the destruction of Sodom and Gomorrah. If either one of those places had been destroyed by sand, say, the slow erosion of the Sahara, they might have believed. But not by fire, for the reasons already mentioned.

And, must it be said? The constants in both cases were absent women, or, as the Ibo liked to deflect such things, women's absence. To which they cry, "Pudenda, pudenda," whenever such stories are told, the name referring simultaneously to shame and female parts.

There existed in the tribe at that time an atavist named Libidoki, a male by smell and inclination, but a creature so low on the evolutionary ladder that he was often overlooked at census-taking or any other civilized activity. No one knew who the parents of Libidoki had been. He lived along the ground, moving himself at snail's pace by digging into the dirt with his hairy hands. The closest he came to an upright carriage was an occasional up-lifting to all fours, on knees and elbows, for the purpose of defecating or sexing with stones.

In Libidoki the sense of smell prevailed above all others. In the manner of processional ants, he secreted saliva, sweat and urine on everything he touched or butted against or mounted, using the smells of these salvos to guide him. His diet consisted mostly of insects: click beatles, dors, elaters. Once in awhile, he finished off the carcass of some animal, after the lions and hyenas had done with it. He, himself, smelled like water buffalo, after they have worked up a heavy sweat.

His one show of social awareness was in his short-lived fascination with the game of basketball. Of course, he liked the smell of the leather and tried to eat the ball. And he could not square up enough to handle the bounce, so he was forever called for double-dribbling. But he was adept at drawing the charge and causing opponents to leave the game altogether with fits of nausea. He gave up the game because, it was surmised, he got tired of getting his hands stepped on.

Adults wanted nothing to do with him, but children were fascinated with him, taunting him with grub worms and glue. They made up rhymes about him, and he in turn seemed to be essaying to communicate with them as well in the few guttural utterances he could manage. The following exchange was typical.

"Libidoki, in your mouth the tse-tse flies are buzzin'."

". . . grrmmm . . . eat me . . . spasm . . ."

"Your kaka comes out by the dozen."

". . . frrnnnk . . . coit . . . sskk . . . chasm . . ."

"To toads and lepers you are cousin."

". . . ssppt . . . pus . . . eeah . . . plasm . . ."

In this way the children served a purpose, in the maintenance of a limited vocabulary in Libidoki. And he served a purpose as well, by deferring in the children the clarity of being cut off in their earliest object-relations.

Libidoki's repeated attempts to mount sleeping women necessitated a constant vigil in the tribe, which was not difficult since his smell preceded him so ferociously. But some of the men of the tribe wanted to have done with the creature who knew nothing of repression. Lon Nol Lumumba once sprayed the limited pasture grass with pesticides, but he only succeeded in killing off several head of

39

cattle. Libidoki ingested the infirm grass with no apparent side-effects. A lifetime of tree bark, grub worms and insidious beetles had prepared his gastrointestinal track for just such an exigency. Some of the women tried to trick him into the Niger River Delta for bathing, but he would not go in. It wasn't that he was afraid of water. It was rather that the water offered no smell-seduction for him. Brother Jero suggested that he be sent on a lorry to the Maryknoll missionaries in Lagos for a long-term Christian education, but this solution was dropped after Libidoki ate a rosary and defecated the beads of the Sorrowful Mysteries. Apparently, they were stuck with him, and yet the incidence of attempted mountings had reached scandalous proportions.

"What if he should succeed one day?" Ngugi asked Kimbene, his king.

"Sensate particulars."

"No, I jest not," Ngugi said.

"Then we would have to deal with the tragedy of offspring."

"We might better nip the problem in the bud."

This was code for castration and Kimbene knew it. Even the idea of it was anathema to him.

"You can take the fox out of the chicken coop," Kimbene said, "but that will not erase the hen from the dream of the fox."

Analogies to dreams were always poignant in sticky problems of state.

"But Libidoki might not even feel the loss of it. Do you think he even knows what he is doing when he voids himself that way?"

"Better than knowing. He feels what he is doing. Which one of us can say as much?"

"Semantics, my dear fellow. What if this were one of your stool wives in question?"

That question, ending with the word question, put another question in Kimbene's mind, the kind of creative question he would not have gotten to by reason alone, and for which he was glad, but he did not share it with Ngugi.

"Still, we must exhaust all the possibilities, Ngugimahn. What other problems of government have we?"

"We have a hunger problem. No sugar cane. No rice crop."

"Begin rationing at once. Tell Brother Jero to accept more of the young for schooling in Lagos. They are the big eaters. What else can we do?"

"Declare an end to all feasting?"

"The people shall remember the feasting long after they have forgotten the famine. What else?"

"Make war on the Edo and steal their crop."

"I am not against the idea of a local war. Hunger makes a good soldier."

"That is all, then. Unless you have any problems to speak of."

"Naomi. I have this problem: what to do with Naomi. Do I have certain rights as her king and husband?"

"Of course you do."

"Do I have divine rights?"

"What do you mean?"

"*Le droit du seigneur* and all such."

41

"You have been doing your reading, Kimbene, mahn. She still resists you?"

"Worse. She has taken to writing. She is keeping a diary."

"This is unheard of. You must discourage this."

"I put her in charge of the fire. I thought it would tire her. Instead, when we go to the darkness in which I cannot see, she still has the fire in her eyes and writes."

"Do you think she writes about absence?"

"I fear so."

"You must find a way to penetrate her, once and for all."

"Maybe in Shakespeare you can help me find a way."

"I will sleep on it."

Left alone, Kimbene began to wonder about the nature of things. On the one hand, Libidoki was a problem for an excess of mounting. On the other hand, Naomi was a problem for lack of mounting. Could all of life's problems be reduced to this, then? Mounting? And he wondered further. He had two stool wives who were getting fat with pregnancy and one stool wife who was getting lean with denial. How was it that the one who denied him pained him far more than the two who surrendered to him pleased him? He began to think that human beings were no different from animals in terms of pleasure and that human beings differed from other human beings only in their capacity to feel pain. This was a radical notion, so radical that he wondered if he hadn't read it somewhere, which prompted him to wonder how it was that one could mistake something one read with the feeling that one had authored it. He, too, went to sleep on these matters and others besides, but he was kept awake long into the night by the sound of scrawling, some kind of primitive writing with absence at its origin, like the sound of an animal scratching, preparing to pounce.

In the days that followed, Kimbene yielded to mounting pressure in the Libidoki affair and agreed to the introduction of pornography for the purpose of trick-therapy. Lurid photos of naked women, many in fragmented close-ups of exposed breasts, butts and hairy aeries, were strewn about the surroundings in the manner of poster-portraits before a political election. The hope was that the hedonistic Libidoki would lay waste to the bold images and leave off of live women. In fact, the incidence of unwanted teenage pregnancies rose, while the pictures had no effect on Libidoki whatsoever because they lacked the olfactory stimuli necessary to his ejaculation. When indeed he took notice of the photographs at all, which was rarely, he merely crawled across them, experiencing only enough tickling at the wrinkling of glossy paper to micturate, salivate or leave a fetid ball of offal. And the tribe, represented by Brother Jero and the Board of Interviews, came to complain to Kimbene, not because of the unwanted pregnancies, which were after all subconsciously wanted, nor because of the piles of excreta, which merely pasturized the streets and yards, but because of the high prevalence of horseflies, maggots, mosquito larva and head lice occasioned by the offal, which, while awful, was not unlawful.

All seemed lost when a miracle occurred in the form of an unexpected visit to the tribe by a Finnish soap dealer, called a *saippuakauppias*. No one in the tribe, and least of all Perry Lumumba, had ever experienced a noun that long and still palindromic, but "soap dealer" in Finnish was just such a word, and so they attended to him as though to a messiah.

Kimbene invited both Libidoki and the *saippuakauppias* to a royal supper. The plan, formulated by Ngugi, was to dull the senses of Libidoki with familiarity and excessive palm wine so that the next morning, still agrog, he would be susceptible to an aerial attack from the Finn, who would douse Libidoki with disinfectant, soap lather, and certain secret ingredients, like salt-peter, known to inhibit sexuality in its very aim.

"What kind of soap have you brought, Finn?" Kimbene asked his guest.

"Why, Ivory, of course, so named for your coast."

He answered the rural royal question, but he kept his eyes on the stool wives: on Stella and Della, who were stuffing themselves with rice cakes and marinated oxen strips, and on Naomi, who was not eating at all.

"We know about soap, you know," Kimbene said. "We make it ourselves."

"Is that so?" the *saippuakauppias* said.

"Yes. West African palm oil, the color of yams and sweet potatoes; fertile white vegetable shortening in forty-pound chunks; clumps of cocoa butter and shavings of beeswax—all mixed in a potlatch of burnt wood."

"I am impressed."

And the squat Ngugi, also wishing to impress the soap dealer, said the following:

"Indeed, we are not surprised by the idea of setting up the use of soap as an actual yardstick to civilization."

"I dare say that deodorant might be a better yardstick," the soap dealer said, rubbing his eyes as he spoke.

In fact, his eyes had not stopped tearing since he first set foot in their midst.

"Are you sad?" Della asked him.

"No, mam. Merely stench-whipped."

"Don't eat with your fingers, Stella," Kimbene admonished his first stool wife.

"Libidoki does," Stella said, pouting.

It was true. Libidoki was feasting upon cow chips and ox-gristle with much moaning, masticating, belching and regurgitation. His thick fingers glistened with grease.

"Libidoki is not the yardstick here and I am your ruler," Kimbene said. "We have a white man here, our guest. An Aryan. Do you want him to form false impressions?"

"I want him to fondle my love-button," Stella said.

Stella could be incredibly provocative when it came to strangers. For this reason Ngugi had opposed her stoolwifery, but he had been overruled.

"How long is your fetish?" Della asked the foreigner.

"I dare say, I don't think I have one."

"This can be rectified," Ngugi said, still trying to play the gracious host.

"This reminds me of a joke, soapmahn," Kimbene said. "What's the difference between a lady in church and a lady in the bathtub?"

"I haven't even the foggiest."

"One has hope in her soul," Kimbene said, doubling over and cracking up with laughter, so that he was unable to complete the joke. When he righted himself, he noticed that Libidoki was laughing along with him, a kind of deep and leechy-devious laughter one more normally associates with hyena, crows and frogs during mating season. Kimbene threw him a garlic clove, which Libidoki ingested and which shut up his laughter immediately.

After supper Ngugi produced music by Sibelius, to which Stella slam-danced with the *saippuakauppias*, picking his pocket in the process.

That night, while everyone slept, Kimbene covered himself with wet flour and sugar cane paste, to which he adhered horsehair, garlic cloves and fresh excreta. Thus did he steal into his own tent, mount and penetrate the unsuspecting Naomi from behind, stuffing her mouth with stones so that she could not speak. He made his escape by covering Naomi in fishing net, so that she could not follow him. Then he ran to the river, washed himself in

46

Finnish soap and hurried back to the tent of Stella, where he pretended sleep and waited for Naomi to come to him with the story of her violation.

But she never came.

Instead, she sought out Libidoki at the sun's first light, and with inducements of body smells she steered him to the river, where she climbed a tree whose branches extended over the water's edge. Libidoki followed her scent to the embankment and stopped. For the first time in his life sight replaced smell in his mind's screen. He could see the maiden shimmering upon the water. Perched thus at the threshold of civilization, he pushed himself up on all fours, allowed his penis to erect itself, lurched forward and summarily drowned.

Pleased with herself, Naomi went back to her tent, wrote about her experience and slept, even as everyone else was getting up.

"So? Where is he that is my work?" the soap dealer asked.

"Vanished," Kimbene said. "Your mere presence has caused his disappearance. We are accustomed to such things in Africa."

"Then I must be getting back to Lagos."

"Go with our blessings," Ngugi said.

"Go with our blessings," Stella said.

"I hope it's a boy," he said back to her.

"Inter urinas et faeces nascimur," Ngugi said.

"Egad. An adage," Perry Lumumba said.

"Hey, Finn," Kimbene said. "Say hi to Tom and Becky. And tell Jim we love him best."

47

The Finnish soap dealer left, shaking his head.

Kimbene could not have been more pleased with himself. He was grateful to Libidoki, wherever he went.

VI

There comes a time when, humor aside, events seem to take over, with a life of their own, an avalanche effect, and powerful people are powerless to stop them. At such a time the minimalism of contrivance ebbs and falls away, like the sloughed skin of a snake, to be replaced by venom, a virile cruelty, and voices that either echo mindlessly or roar. One feels suddenly both the urgency and the dislocation of living a double life: the linear day, with all the surreptitious trappings of any other day, and a larger history, the monstrous bloody mouth of history, ready to devour anything in its path. Such a cataclysmic time often commences with a trifle, a thing that could have been avoided, but which, having happened, causes two other things, themselves avoidable, except that the causality between them and the first thing is always hidden, and they then create five other things which finally have a life of their own, which means that logic fails, reasons run amok, and people are no longer capable of tracing events back to their origins. So, they make war instead.

And time, itself, is on the side of the warring parties, not with the pacifists. The rural king Kimbene, faced with a famine due to his own excesses at feasting, had already decided to make war on the neighboring Edo when they made war on him instead. Kimbene had enlisted his friend Ngugi to find reasons to justify expansion, evening incursions for the purpose of stealing food, daytime defensive postures of fortification and singing patriotic songs. And Ngugi had not failed him. He had a speech ready. He was going to propose to the tribe the narcissism of minor differences, a concept so succinct and subtle that it could not be repudiated. Just as the mirror never really gives a true reflection, but always involves a distortion or reversal of the image, so too the Ibo and Edo were not really that much alike, even though they shared common boundaries, similar crops, interchangeable dialects, even stool wives. This was to be his argument. The war, far from being a hostile act, was rather to be seen as a clarification of nuances, a subtle delineation of differences, and, of course, the chance to eat again.

But he never got to give his speech, because the Edo attacked first. Now, had Kimbene been truly innocent in his thinking, he would have assumed the posture of the wronged party and gone to the Edo, by means of some delegation—Brother Jero

and the Board of Interviews were already in place
for such a contingency—to explain the rightness
and wrongness of small claims, local grief, civil
torts. But he had it in mind to attack the Edo and
so he felt guilty and exposed when they attacked
first, and rather than search for reasons why they
might attack in the first place, he merely welcomed
the war as a *fait accompli* and was glad not to have
to justify it.

And yet the wonder persists, outside of time and
in inverse proportion to the constriction and fer-
vent pressing of the time, how such a border war
gets started. Imagine, then, the following scenario.
A man lives in a hamlet which has no name and
nor do any of the neighboring hamlets have a name
or fence or flag or any other identifying marks. One
day he sees a stray cow and he is hungry. It might
have been a ratel, ferret, eland, emu or gnu, but
these are too exotic for our purposes, and so the
stray must be a potentially domesticated beast for
there to be any presumed ownership to support a
tort. So, it's a stray cow and the man is hungry. His
first thought is not of the ownership of the animal.
His second thought is not of the ethics involved.
His third thought is not of the possibility of getting
away undetected. And, must it be said, his fourth
thought is not of the consequences of his action. He
is merely hungry, and so he dismisses all these non-
thoughts that never happened and any other
thoughts which would likewise deny or defer his
hunger. He slaughters the cow. Maybe he eats a
piece, a raw piece, a little silly slab of beef, the

equivalent of a sandwich. Maybe he skins the carcass and hides the bones or buries them. Maybe he enlists the vultures in his enterprise and takes some Catholic solace in feeding the birds, who neither till nor tarry long. And he takes a whole bloody side of beef home with him and says it's wild boar. If they are hungry enough, they will believe him.

But, supposing this was the last cow of a diminished herd, due to disease or feasting or loss of pasture grass, and this cow strayed because it, too, was hungry. Imagine the wrath of the farmer who follows the birds of prey to the place where the carcass lies and feels the loss of his last hope of farming, which intensifies his own hunger, which feeds his rage. Would not he be of a mind to carve a slab of meat, say, an arm or a leg, from the one who killed his cow, regardless of territorial boundaries?

Perhaps morality requires that we first imagine a scenario of need, when in fact there was no need at all, but simply a case of idleness, which afflicts human beings, grabs them and will not let go, until they are ready to fight to the death for non-vital means. Perhaps it was a matter of non-vital whimsy, pure and simple, like sugar. Imagine a man with his machete, working in the canebrakes all his life. A solitary life, full of cloaked awareness, surrounded by shoots of sugar cane, a life of stooping and bending and, most of all, hacking, the machete his only way of getting in or out of the labyrinthine brakes, his only means of seeing the light. Imagine such a man, for whom hacking has become as second-nature as spitting or sleeping or micturating. But for some reason this man is not hacking. Maybe the brakes have all bent over in failure, due to some blight or pestilence, neglect or too much feasting, and suddenly there is more visibility than he has ever experienced before. And in his field of vision, he spots another man, where before he had never seen a man, only shoots, and he is transfixed, avoyeuring. Of course he has seen another man before, but never in this circumstance, in which the other man does not see him, and he has only to watch, his machete idle in his hand, the habit of hacking still uppermost among his motor skills. And suddenly he begins to wonder this strange and silly thought: what if I were to hack this man with my machete, in lieu of the cane? Am I able? And, before he knows it, he is. Maybe he beheads the man on the first circular swatch. Or maybe he aims lower and cuts a belt of blood around the man's waist. Or maybe he tries for a transversal cut at the back of the knees, like a clip in football. Wherever he cuts, it is not done out of need, but rather because it feels good to be hacking again. And cutting through a taboo is sweeter than bamboo or cutting pure and simple sugar cane. And thus begins a border war.

The sun, itself, has been blamed in more than one instance for its blinding light, when someone fired four times, at point-blank range, into the face of the nearest Bedouin passerby.

But enough of allusions and back to our proto-narratives, which are equally illuminating, if however less blinding. Need and idleness have already

53

been proposed as possible scenarios. But what about cruelty? Suppose an Edo man spots an Ibo man in a clearing in the canebrakes. This Edo man has heard of all the non-stop feasting among the Ibo. He wonders at such wealth and suffers from envy, for there has been no feasting among his tribe. And so he suddenly espies an Ibo man in a clearing, and that man is not working. That man is in a crouch, a kind of defecatory crouch, except that he is not voiding. No, he is eating a banana or plantain. Worse, he takes his time, he savors each bite, and the white of the banana has crowded his teeth and left a kind of cake around his lips. The banana is long and hard, curved just so and incredibly white. The Edo man experiences a localized envy. And can there be any worse kind than that? He begins to sweat, watching the Ibo man eat with such relish, such candor, such *je ne sais quoi* physicality. Maybe the Edo man depersonalizes the Ibo man, strips him of a soul, such things have happened, and by way of a trope he sees the Ibo man as some kind of monkey eating a banana with a kind of bon-vivant animal elan denied human beings. Or perhaps the Edo man feels his focus only on the banana, whose powers of provocation are unmatched among fruits. Maybe the Edo man is hungry. Maybe he feels insulted. Maybe he thinks the Ibo man is mocking him, even though there is no ostensible proof that the Ibo man is even aware of the other's existence. Maybe there is a moment of lost virility for the Edo, who has had no feasting. And maybe, just maybe, he is distracted by temperament: he is a poor worker, he has no need of a trope, he is someone who looks for an occasion to be cruel. Such a man does not come out of the brakes and into the clearing to share a last bite on a banana. No. Instead he circles the clearing, dousing the sugar cane shoots with liquor or linseed oil or any other flammable mixture. And then he sets the field on fire. He hides himself, for it would not do to be seen, and he listens for the screams. He closes his eyes and imagines the banana burning inside the Ibo man's stomach. Maybe he joins in with those who have come to put out the fire. He feels an aliveness beyond food or drink, sleep or sex.

As protonarratives go, this one is perhaps the least likely and the most compelling, which ratio is often true, whatever the civilization in question. Following this ratio, we are obliged to look at one last protonarrative, interesting only for its particularity.

A little Edo boy named Tyree was told by a shaman of his tribe that he could slay his father and marry his mother, but he refused such prophecy and gave himself over to voyeurism rather than direct action. One day while walking in the brush, or bush, as even African authors have taken to calling it, he espied two snakes mating, and he was changed into a little girl for seven years. During that time he was taught the secret arts of keeping a fire and writing, for which he was grateful, but he was also taught more menial skills, like sharpening spears, adding lentils to oxen broth, nose-piercing for the purpose of wearing bones, and sitting, hours on end of sitting, on the outside chance that he might be chosen as a stool wife one day. He tried to play basketball, but he was eschewed. He tried to micturate upon the campfire, but only succeeded in shaming his own legs. He tried telling tall tales, but nobody would listen. He was still of one mind, but of another body.

Seven years later, he chanced upon the same two snakes mating, for they are faithful creatures, doomed to monogamy by their hideous skins and habits, and he was changed back into a male again, albeit one with a high-pitched voice and a predilection for exchanging recipes during rituals. His parents experienced a form of scarce-belief at hearing where he had been all that time, which was right under their noses. They concluded that puberty had been a bit too much for him, and they believed not at all the part about the snakes. When news of his adventure reached his rural king, a tall man named Friday, Tyree was asked to referee an altercation between Friday and his stool wives. The stool wives claimed that their king had wandering looks and was oversexed, to which Friday responded by saying that women got more pleasure from sex than men, and so it was only right and just that men should compensate by getting more sex than women. Tyree, who had been in both bodies, ruled in favor of his king. In anger one of the stool wives smote him blind. King Friday could not reverse such a royal punishment, but he could reward by compensation, and so he declared that Tyree should be his personal dreamspeaker, a lofty position with very few duties. Still, Tyree's parents were not satisfied and they pressed for the truth, which is to say, a story they might believe. At long last, Tyree told them he had been abducted by the Ibo, beaten and tortured, and made to wear dresses for seven years. With this new tale in his ears, Friday still could not give him back his sight, but he could make war on the Ibo as compensation.

So go the tall tales, faster than the crow can fly from baobab to baobab, and the final truth is never as important as the least of its embellished variations. And it is time to say that none of these non-scenarios ever occurred to Kimbene, who was so grateful that the Edo had attacked, for whatever reason, that he wanted to mount his counterattack before they changed their minds. And, amidst all the preparations for war—putting lurid make-up on and fine-tuning darts and spears—there came to Kimbene a foreign correspondent from Lagos, an Italian journalist named Caruso.

"Why are you here?" Kimbene asked point-blank, having no time for ceremonial hospitality.

"It was said in Lagos that the Edo decimated your tribe, that they used poison gas and made your women and children watch the beheading of your men, and there was talk of cannibalism to boot, as we say in Italia. So, I decided to go to the underdog, to interview the last survivors."

"As you can see, we are all quite well and fine."

"And, of course, we are all grateful for that. But

may I tag along when you go to battle? I need a story to justify my trip, and the Edo will certainly not respect my press pass now."

"I am not in the habit of staging spectacles for foreign journalists."

"Il lupo perdie su pelo ma non su vizio."

"What is this tally-talk?"

"Just a saying we have about habit. So, how about it?"

"On one condition. If you die, I will not count you as a casualty for our side."

"Fair enough. Which way to the front?"

"Sit with my stool wives. We are not prepared to go just yet."

Following the advice of the wise Ngugi, Kimbene had ordered a counting of the entire tribe, so that they could ascertain how many had fallen. After many hours of count and recount, it was concluded that everyone was present. Apparently, no one had fallen at the hands of the Edo.

"Below and hold," Kimbene began in his deepest baritone.

"That's 'lo and behold,' " Ngugi whispered in his ear.

"Lo and behold," Kimbene began again, "we are truly pre-lapsarian. None of us has fallen. How can this be when the Edo have already attacked and bombard us with casualty count?"

"It's a dirty sneaking low-down Edo trick," Lon Nol Lumumba said.

"Add lies to evil," his brother Idi said.

"Edo ode," Perry Lumumba said.

"Yes, fool," Kimbene said. "They fabricate a poesy. But why? We must ask the wise Ngugi."

"A battle took place," Ngugi said. "We have witnesses who saw the carnage. But, since we have no dead, I must posit the following: the Edo came in two parties, one to look like them, another to look like us. Then they slaughtered the ones who looked like us."

"But surely they knew that we would have a counting and discover this trick?"

"Alas, yes. But we are left confused and certainly not mentally competent to wage a war. In such a state we will surely lose."

"So we must comprehend the ploy?"

"Adamantly," Ngugi said.

"What do you suppose, Ngugimahn?"

"That they had excess population, for one thing."

"Clever, that. But, then, are Edo warriors in such abundance?"

"Maybe they were women, dressed to look like warriors."

"This would support your theory of excess population."

"Yes, and if we thought they had so many warriors that some were expendable?"

"Then we would be demoralized, for we have no way of taking a counting of their tribe."

"So, what do you conclude, Kimbene?"

"That we are matched against an admirable foe.

But, if they could rely on us figuring out the trick, then how could they be sure we wouldn't reason the rest?"

"It doesn't matter," Ngugi said. "If we didn't, then we were left confused. If we did, then we were left to admire. Either way, they have a decided advantage."

"What can we do about that?"

"We must either confuse them or make them admire us. These are apparently the rules of war."

"We can adapt to such rules," Kimbene said. "This is called targeting the market, then marketing the target."

"If you wish," Ngugi said, deferring to the occasional doltish comment from his king.

"I must sleep on this," Kimbene said. "Yes, thus will we confuse the Edo. No sentries. No watchtower. No sorties. No counterattack. Just the appearance of deep sleep in every tent. But within, one male warrior must stay awake in each tent. I will stay awake in mine. Your king will sleep on this and emerge with a plan to make them admire us. I have some knowledge of admiration. Caruso, you must sleep out here with the fire like a common animal. The Edo can see you and know we dare to expend a white man."

"Zis is too much, no?" Caruso complained. "At least, you canna give me a white flag, no? A Red Cross flag, yes?"

"No, tally-talker," Kimbene said. "We can't have any show of weakness. Mercy is the butter on cruelty's toast."

"And weakness the marmalade," Lon Nol Lumumba said.

With that, they all retired to sleeping and vigilance, the two like the stripes of the zebra.

Outside, near the dying embers of the fire, Caruso began to pen his day's dispatch to *Il Figaro* in Rome.

"I know what Ayla must have felt long ago, to be shunned by the Cave Bear. I am alone, in the middle of a terrible war of attrition, a war that makes no sense at all. All around me, the sounds of restless animals in the bush. They seem to know what is happening. This could be the Vietnam of the Ibo, the Angola of the Edo. Neither side knows the actual boundaries that separate one tribe from the other. Why don't they build a fence?"

He put his tape recorder down, because he remembered that he had forgotten to take his malaria pills. But at that moment Stella, the first stool wife, emerged from her tent. She began to give suck to Mike, her newborn child.

"You have incredible breasts," Caruso said.

"Yes, two of them."

"Yes, of course. Why you no can sleep?"

"I want to learn about Roma. This smells good to me."

"Do you have any brandy?"

"No, I have only mother's milk."

"No matter. I can tella the story sober, I sink so. Long ago there were these two bambini, name a Romulus and Remus, and they sucka the tit of they mama, jus' like you, only she was a wolf."

Thus began another protonarrative, with whose origins and many variations we are already familiar.

At the same time, deep within the royal tent, Kimbene was trying to think up a way to trick the Edo into admiring him and his tribe. However, his third stool wife Naomi wanted more initiations into the ways of the flesh. For his part, Kimbene thought it strange how conjugal life often mirrors the life of the tribe. Stella had given birth to Mike and Della had given birth to Moustafa. Both were healthy babies, sons and would-be kings one day. They might have been satisfied, except that their king and husband now ignored them completely and spent most of his stool-wife time with the barren Naomi. They had become intensely jealous of Naomi, the third stool wife, who was being treated like a first stool. Their reasoning was sound. They had produced sons, as they were supposed to do, so why was she who produced nothing getting all the attention and amorous advances? Was it because she had long resisted him who advanced?

Little did they know that her time of resistance had long passed, and she was now as eager as she formerly was reluctant. She had apparently come to understand one of the basic secrets of eroticism, at least as they concern men. If you greatly resist a man, he will come back. If you boldly go forth and show him passion he has not seen before, he will come back. Stella and Della had fallen somewhere in between those two extremes, somewhere at the neuter point. They neither resisted much nor gave themselves overmuch. They got pregnant and gave birth, for which they received the approval of the whole tribe. But they had not gained the love and respect of Kimbene.

That night in the tent, Kimbene tried to resist Naomi.

"I must think of a plan. A man, a plan, your love canal. No, I must not think this way."

Naomi smothered his feet with kisses and rubs, the deep squeeze of which he felt all the way to his brain.

"The Edo do not sex this night. Of this I am sure."

Naomi smothered his knees and inner thighs with kisses, small bites and pinches, which pressure he felt all the way to his chest and stomach.

"What would Ngugi say if he saw me this way, utterly without a plan?"

Naomi smothered his loincloth with longing, using her tongue like a castanet, which clicking and clacking he felt all the way into his abdomen, bowels and groin.

"You are erect," she whispered.

"Yes, the shame of it."

"Come to bed and I will tell you a joke with my body. It will make you laugh all over, I promise you."

One thing is true of men, even men of state. Once they are aroused, they cannot be anything else. Ice goes to water, water goes to steam. Kimbene was at the vapor stage.

"You are hard as a fetish," she flattered him.

"Beat it, then," he said, carrying her to the bed.

63

Toes to toes, legs to legs, belly to belly, they matched and were different, they danced and were alone, they trembled and made an uncontrollable calm between them. Sexing, like feasting, has many meanings. The miracle of melting, one to two, two to one, was that they were the same height horizontally. The vertical world became a lax memory in their skins, as they perched and whirled, arched and shoved, all manner of movements reduced to one movement. And they understood the adage of their elders: to pitch ten tents, one needs but one peg. Naomi understood that she would never have to fit in. Her name now was secure upon her king's lips, which was the same as history. And Kimbene understood that he would come away from this night with the knowledge of fire and women and writing, and how absence completed all of these.

The joke she told him was this: what is sex backwards? Kimbene thought immediately of his fool Lumumba, and his mouth clicked with k and g, trying to pronounce the x, and the clicking sound was followed by sees or seas or some likewise vast and docile sound. But Naomi laughed and turned her whole body around, until she was fully exposed to him. And he understood and laughed throughout the rest of that night.

VII

I am the crown-king Kimbene, and I hold dominion over certain places, certain peoples and certain
things. Now I hold dominion over language as
well, for in Africa words are the last things to be
owned. We master the body first, then food, rituals,
politics. Finally, there is literacy. I who have always
known how to boast and toast, to wield weapons
and tell tall tales, now have learned an alphabet, a
limited mastery of writing. Now I have proof of
memory. The past has always been promiscuous.
Now it is not. The future has always been a
guarded thing, a matter for clairvoyance. Now it is
not. The present is less direct. So be it.

After great sex a formal feeling comes, and this
is my time of formal feelings. You cannot undress
a piece of writing the way you can a speaking. Writing requires more respect, a delicacy, an extended
courtship. You must woo the words before you can

undress them. Before I knew how to write, I wanted feasting, many servants and stool wives, money and comfort. Now that I can see what I have said on paper, I want power. I want to be a king that crows, a scourge upon the land. Before, I showed mercy out of ignorance. Now I can be cruel by calculation. If I cannot find a quote in books to justify me, I will invent one and quote myself. This is the power of the alphabet.

I was not meant to be king. I was not born to it nor groomed for it nor encouraged in any way to dream this dream, that my height would one day surpass all others. I was never a prince. Listen, let me tell you about kings in my country. The rural king sexes a stool wife, and a baby results, but not without much ceremony and expectation. The whole tribe waits, denied any vision of the actual event. Listen, it is like the smoke of Popes. If a flag moves in a circle, the tribe knows the baby is a girl. If it stands still at an angle of ninety degrees, then it's a boy.

But this is not just any weak and pouty boy. He is not allowed to be a baby. To constrict the crying of this baby, he is gagged with a special linen, and an inch-long golden wand is placed in one of his hands as a symbol of sovereignty, and also to tighten his fists from the very first breath.

As he grows this boy is coddled in many ways, beaten and restricted in other ways. For example, he is constantly pelted with stones at the joints, to insure that he speeds to maturity faster than his contemporaries, thereby gaining the height advantage. He is given food to eat, where other children must wait behind their mothers for scraps thrown by the men.

At the age of twenty-one his head is shaved of all hair. The blood of a lamb and five bottles of Schnapps are poured beneath his stool. And he retires to the golden stool, away from all publicities, where he is given the divine, enough divinity to rule his tribe. Once he is enstooled, he is allowed to eat and dance in public, speak in dialects and drive an ordinary car. He is therefore always visible to his people. He is expected to be clairvoyant, especially so in foreseeing wars to come, so that his warriors can be prepared and never lose in battle. He sexes his stool wives, hopes for male children, and sees that the order is followed again. This is his immortality.

He may believe in ghosts and dreams or he may not. He may sometimes dress Best Western or he may not. He may be kind to missionaries or he may kill them. There are no prescribed rules for such things. His height is his birthright, his stool is his blessing.

I was not born to silver spoons and a golden stool. No flags announced my coming, nor was I gagged with linen or pelted at the joints for growth. My father was a palm wine drunkard who left for Lagos when it was discovered my mother was pregnant. He hadn't the heart to see me born. And my mother hadn't the strength to birth me. My birth was her death, the two moments mixed until they were the same moment. I was a curse upon them both.

I was raised by strangers, in a family that already included six children. And while my borrowed father cared very little for me, my borrowed mother saw in me, her seventh child, a magical boy, and she was determined not to see me starve to death, even to the point of procuring food for me before her own six boys, who despised me mightily.

The procurement of food is symptomatic of everything that is good and bad about the African family. Listen, let me tell you about African diets and kitchens and you will see what I mean. We have tried to diversify, to keep from starving to death. Growing rice and sugar cane are new. Breeding cow or pig is new. Goat and ox are more traditional. So is cassava, which is a root, a tuber, like the potato is a tuber, although I have never seen a potato. The beauty of cassava is that it grows everywhere. In that respect it is like a weed. It grows in sun or shade, in sand or dirt, in desert drought or tropical rainforest. There is no stopping it. There is no trick to cassava farming. When someone is particularly useless in our tribe, we say that he or she has found a new way to grow cassava.

The bad part about cassava is that it is poisonous in its natural state. It must be harvested, then boiled, then beaten constantly and violently before it is edible. My mind has a picture of African women, not unlike the picture Best Western tourists carry away with them, with their heads bowed, standing, working all their muscles downward, working with something like mortar and pestle, beating the cassava day in and day out, as though it were a plague of locusts, until it could be eaten.

Variety of kitchen is a new concept in Africa. Traditionally, there was only one meal to be eaten, the evening meal. And that meal consisted of cassava, pieces of which were dipped in a hot and spicy sauce, and the trick was to gather up the few pieces of sliced goat or egg at the top, because otherwise one was eating only starch and sauce, starch and watery sauce. And what was left over from the one meal was served again at the next meal until that entire batch of cassava was used up, and then there was a new batch served.

My first Minister Ngugi has told me that in Europe and America there are restaurants, and in those restaurants there are cards called menus, which list many different kinds of meats, tubers, sauces and other extraordinary foods which are not poisonous, which are kept fresh and which are truly available, and not just listed for tall tales or ornamental value. This is an amazement to me. I want some day to go abroad and see this thing.

But back to our native kitchens. Traditionally in African tribes, the men eat first and by themselves around the fire. They boast and toast, they brag and are wasteful. Maybe they are eating the meat of the goat or an occasional chicken, and when they get near the bone they toss it over their shoulders into the darkness. But the darkness is crowded with women who wait to catch such bones. Sometimes they eat for themselves. Sometimes they pass a small piece of gristle or bone to the children, who wait behind them. This is what my borrowed mother did for me. She held me up above her own six sons and fed me near her face, where they couldn't grab the bone away. This is how I grew to be seven feet tall today.

And this is, then, the hierarchy in all the Africas: first, the grown men, because they are the warriors; then the grown women, because they keep the fires and stamp the cassava and feed the men and sometimes sex them; and finally the children, who have, after all, a limited value. If a child starves and dies, we can always make another.

Ngugi has told me that in Europe and America this order is reversed. The children are coddled and protected by laws. They are made to feel, however falsely, that the world is theirs. Then come the women, because they are considered weaker than the men. And then come the grown men, who have very limited value. According to Ngugi, there is nothing more despised in these cultures than an old man, because he has ceased to be useful to women and he is too distanced from children. This, too, is an amazement to me.

In order to be rural king, I tricked the wily Joe Odoki at the baobab tree. Joe Odoki was wily and wise, but he had no luck with children. All his died of disease or starvation, so he was left without a line. Thus, the next rural king was going to come from outside the royal family anyway, and I felt no moral cramps being the one to step in those shoes.

If I let feasting go on too long, it was because I had no better plan and knew no better thing to do than to show by excess the plenty of my potentate. And when I was told that all our crops were failing and there was no new food to feast, yet I feasted, with tall tales of bravery and magic and contrived clairvoyance, because hunger was not a new crisis, but rather the way things have always been, and so there was no need to address the situation in any frantic way. In fact, I let women come out of the darkness and occasionally feed with the men. I have kept my stool wives closer to the fire than any other rural king I know. And I have sometimes fed some scraggly-ribbed children with my own personal plate, not because I knew it would do them any good in the long hall of hungry life, but because I derived some pleasure in prolonging their agony. Death is, after all, not so different from a full stomach, in that both still the screaming inside the body. Nor did I feed them indiscriminately. For example, I never gave food to a tall boy. This would be folly.

I have finally sexed my third stool wife Naomi, the formerly nihilistic Naomi, who has always had more truck with the dead than with the living. I used to think of her as the negation of a negation, but I find I was near-death wrong about her. There is a waterfall of longing in her I can barely imagine and have yet to get behind. Sluice to a river, her body is an opaque waterway, behind which there is flood. Stella and Della have given me sons. Naomi gives me something else. She gives me what the golden stool was supposed to give: an inkle of the gods.

She resisted me for a temporality or two. I now understand this had nothing to do with me, and everything to do with forced sexing from her father, who has long ago left our tribe to live as a demon in the cities. And when I asked her whatever happened to that urge-lizard Libidoki, she replied: "He sleeps with the fishes." We will keep this secret from the tribe, for secret-keeping is part of the custodial role of rural kings.

And now I am embroiled in an enigmatic war with the Edo, which Ngugi has maintained is the narcissism of minor differences, even though we have no need of reasons to wage a good war. I am told that kings in other cultures look upon war as an interruption, an inconvenience, even a tragedy. From my readings of Best Western books, I find these reasons to be pointillism of the worst sort. Like the frog who must take in hollow air to puff up and expand itself, so too a nation needs a war from time to time to clear its lungs. Besides, we were running out of braveries around the campfire. Besides again, we need a war to distract us from the fact that we are starving. And, although I came up short on clairvoyance, because I did not predict this war, I will compensate with an excellence in rear-ending, which Ngugi calls hindsight.

The trick is this: how can I confuse the Edo and make them admire me? I have the answer, from my long night of excess, of sexing and alphabetting with Naomi. I will write them a letter. I will say:

"Dear Edo Neighbors: How are you? We are exceedingly fine. We are very plural, like the Popes. We have grown so tall we had to get rid of our baobab tree. It no longer measured us. We are still feasting, yawn. It's become a tad tiresome, excuse the Briticism, but someone has to do it. And we are about to name our place. Have you thought of a name for your place? You can have "Pitch Ten Tents," which we considered and then discarded. Come to potlatch sometime, but please, no Biafran jokes. Yours sincerely, Kimbene."

I will send the wordsmithy Caruso with this letter. He is like a fugue. He will return to me, with variations. And, if he doesn't, I will not have lost one of my own warriors. The mailman is far less important than the mail.

It is almost morning. I feel completely juked.

"So, Naomi, what do you think of my writing?"

"You can't spell for lentils, but you are already a passably great penman."

"Thank you for this answer. You are truly my mentor and subject."

VIII

Time passed. A cliche, to be sure, a segue, a transition, just as there is a time in birthing called transition. But time does not pass in Africa the way it does elsewhere. The snapper turtle is an apt metaphor. It budges, it crawls, it slows as it goes, and then it suddenly snaps. In Africa time crawls by like lightning.

Space as well. The white tourists come with tripods and cameras. They want to photograph the animals in the jungle. But the jungle is like a huge umbrella of lianas and vines, baobab trees and ferns. There is no sunlight, no animals to be seen, no path but the path one makes. Space is balmy with sweat by day, cool and impersonal by night. The tourists can smell the animals, but they will never see them.

Anyway, what seemed like temporality passed, and outside the many tents near a dying fire, Della had come to suckle Moustafa, joining Stella and her little Mike, who were both rapt in a slow aspirin trance, listening to Caruso, who in his exposition of the history of Rome had gotten to the Borgia Kings and the Pretender Pope of Avignon.

"I like this one best," Stella said.

"But why?" Caruso begged, a little out of control from too much talking and not enough sleep. "He was niente."

"He is like Remus," Stella said. "The branch that falls off, while the other branch grows. I give homage to these fallen trees."

"History is full of these," Caruso said. "They live for one line and then are caput. Finito, capish?"

"Maybe everybody get to be famous for fifteen temporalities," Della said.

"La fama," Caruso snorted. "Have you got any brandy?" he asked Della.

"No. Only mother's milk."

"Yes, I see. You have beautiful breasts."

"Yes, two of them."

Caruso wondered upon what planet and in what century he had alit. Espresso with Francesca on the Via Veneto seemed frightfully far away. He had come to report on a war, and instead he was reciting the history of Rome to two stool wives who preferred all the secondary characters.

He was saved from such musings when Kimbene emerged from his tent and amassed the whole tribe for another counting.

"I have thought of a way," he said, "to confuse

the Edo and make them admire us. Bring me the blood of a lamb."

"We have eaten all our lamb," Brother Jero said.

"A goat, then."

"We have feasted upon all our goats," Brother Jero said.

"A kid, then."

Lon Nol Lumumba went out and slaughtered a child. He then brought back the blood of the slain boy.

"Not too much trouble?" Kimbene asked.

"No trouble at all," Lon Nol said.

"You see how my wishes are granted," Kimbene said, pouring blood and four bottles of Schnapps under his royal stool. "I have written a letter, which Caruso will deliver to the Edo. They will be confronted and amazed. They will be confused and envious. They will be divided and conquered."

"You musta be kidding," Caruso said.

"This man has learned to speak on a swing," Kimbene said, pointing to Caruso. "You see how he goes up and down, he lilts and elides, he sings when he speaks. He is perfect for our purposes."

Caruso protested that he was a journalist, committed to the impartial reportage of the war, and that he couldn't take a side. Kimbene responded by saying that to deny a royal request would be tantamount to taking a side, the side of the Edo, and that such a denial would be punishable by beheading. The tribe was convinced of the logic in his words, and they began to look silently for tall trees with sturdy branches.

"You will be our Remus," Stella said, inciting him.

"Our Esau," Della said.

"Our Mercurio," Ngugi said.

"Our Last Duchess," Brother Jero said.

"Stab nail at ill Italian bats," Perry Lumumba said.

"It is decided then," Kimbene said. "Caruso goes. And who will know better than a journalist how to report to us their confusion and admiration?"

They dispatched Caruso at spearpoint in the direction of the Edo. Then they reconnoitred, or some facsimile thereof, and listened to their leader.

Stella interrupted him, however, before he could speak.

"What is it, Stella?"

"The tally-talker said we should build a fence."

"This would require much wood, which we need for our fires, and many workers on the picket line, which we do not have. We would only gain a false sense of security, and we would still be defenseless. I have a better way. We must name this place. And since we are not a democracy, I have taken the liberty of naming this place. I have called it——," and he spoke the secret name, which only the members of his tribe should know.

"What about 'Pitch Ten Tents'?" Brother Jero asked.

"I thought of that and discarded it," Kimbene said. "Now we must ready ourselves for battle. The Edo will receive Caruso and think we are waiting for an answer. We must confound them. We will follow the tally-talker at a safe distance through the canebrakes with weapons and willingness. We do not have the foodstuffs for a protracted war, so we will do what we can to make it as short as possible. Remember, the purpose of war is joy. There can be no other reason for expressing so much aggression. So, have a good time of it, boys. And if we should attack and be outnumbered, do not hesitate to run away. We are brave, but we are not stupid. Lastly, as your clairvoyant leader, I should warn you of the unforseen, of which I have much experience from books. I have been reading French guerilla tactics for this. If you are suddenly blinded by the sun, fire your weapon four or five times at point-blank range. It is sure to hit a passerby face. This comes from Camus."

"Camus sees sumac," Perry Lumumba said.

"Let me translate," Kimbene said. "My fool thinks that existentialism was poisoned in its vision of the world. Maybe this is so. But the *situation crise* often arises *a priori*, preceding any analysis of itself. This is the nature of the beast. And so we must defer all further rational debate until we have acted and have something concrete to debate. And so let us go, with this rallying cry I have composed for the occasion: 'Be cruel, be cruel, be true to your stool.' "

Ngugi dared to wonder what stool, but he was the only one. To a man the rest of the warriors had raised their spears on high. They were ready to go kick some Edo coccyx.

War narratives can be wonderfully digressive, because they are, in the main and of necessity, also confrontational. Such narratives allow us to put character, dialogue, plot and point of view in temporary abeyance, and thus to focus on setting, on emotionalizing the terrain, as it were. And so, without further adieu, we switch to that mode.

Kimbene and his band of bellicose warriors moved East, which is to say, left to right. They took pause at the river's edge, cast a rope from one side to the other, and crossed the river in single file, one by one, along the rope, as though it were a cinch. They carried with them flasks of palm wine and potable water, as well as crushed acorns, macademia nuts, mango rinds, pre-shrunken goat strips and other forms of sustenance in the jerky category. They moved cautiously through the dense thickets of ferns, vines and other feral foliage, often walking sideways or backwards, so as not to leave a perceived trail and betray themselves. And when they came to natural obstacles so treacherous that cheetah, puma, leopard and grouse would despair, they forged ahead on winged feet, sacrificing themselves to scratches, rashes, tears and gashes. For example, they ran through the brambles where the rabbits wouldn't go.

And when they came at last to the Edo canebrakes, they fanned out and advanced on all fours, a locus of locusts, a focus of crocus and croquemessieurs. Inch by inch they went, until Kimbene saw before him, in a clearing in the canebrakes, King Friday of the Edo and his own emissary Caruso. Friday and Caruso. Friday was attempting to read the letter Kimbene had scribed, but he read phonetically, halving each word and outloud. There was a mix of confusion and admiration on his dark face. On the face of Caruso there was a mix of boredom, malaise, ennui and *outrance*, all genuine.

Then carefully, ever so carefully, Kimbene emptied a flask of linseed oil and another of French liqueur on the hackneyed canestalks surrounding the clearing. He made as little noise as possible, but of course there was some noise, this minimum of bubbling and caulking and cracking of the parched stalks.

"I hear something," Caruso said.

"Silence," King Friday commanded. "You hear me trying to cipher."

Then Kimbene set the stalks on fire, and he and his men moved backwards like jackdaws, to see the fire, smell the smoke and listen for human screaming.

"Tierra del fuego," he heard Caruso scream.

In the cacophany that ensued, Kimbene couldn't be sure, but he thought he smelled that unmistakable stench of human flesh roasting, blood boiling, bones melting. He was pleased and amazed.

And here an interjection is perhaps in order. Tribes like the Ibo do not require visual proof of atrocities they have committed. In fact, they prefer to imagine such things. And so Kimbene and his men left without a body count, returning to their women and children with many exaggerations of their bravura. They had scratches, rashes, tears and gashes to prove they hadn't been idle. They had smells of the burning bush all over their skins. And they had visible memories of what they had seen and done in their flagrant eyes. Such is war.

Only Naomi remained doubtful of what they had done.

She took it upon herself to quiz Kimbene in the privacy of their tent. This onerous task is called reality-checking.

"What was your rival wearing?"

"He was scantily clad."

"What was he wearing?"

"A loincloth. Some chalky warpaint. Some bones and beads and amulets."

"How do you know the fire was set?"

"I set the fire."

"What color was the fire?"

"Burnt orange. Amber. Terra-cotta."

"How do you know it met with flesh?"

"I smelled a smell that wasn't there before."

"Name this smell."

"We have no equivalents in our kitchens."

"Name it anyway."

"Skunk. Offal. Bitter oleander. Burning dog. Water buffalo sweat."

"And can you say in your heart of hearts that this war is over?"

"No."

"Do you see differently? Is there clairvoyance?"

"No. My fingers itch. My toes tingle. All my extremities squirm. I have tactile clairvoyance."

"How does it express itself?"

"My fingers linger in the future. My toes pose for the past."

"Nothing else?"

"Once in awhile I have olfactory clairvoyance."

"How does it express itself?"

"The nose knows."

He thanked her for this inquisition and concluded that the tribe should remain on red alert: sentries, spies and scouts, every ordinary function lipped with surveillance. They awaited the return of Caruso.

But Caruso did not come back. They had been standing vigil for three lapses of the sun when there wandered into their tribe a young Edo boy named Tyree, who was blind to all appearances.

"I am Tyree, the personal dreamspeaker of the king, although I have very few duties."

"You have the irridescence of opal in your eyes," Kimbene said. "A kind of quartz contentment. The futility of all philosophy. A kind of London fog. Are you really sightless?"

"As bat's wings and bees' wax, your highness."

"Friday's child is full of woe," Ngugi said.

"Like flightless birds," Kimbene said. "You will not mind, lad, if we subject you to a torture or two, to test the veracity of your vision?"

"I was told you would," Tyree said.

A torch was put to his eyes, and, while it singed off his eyebrows and lashes, he did not otherwise blink or flinch.

"His windows are empty," Lon Nol Lumumba said.

"He has found a new way to grow cassava," his brother Bob said.

"Tell us how you came to be so infirm," Kimbene said.

The story of the eye ensued. Tyree told of the twin snakes mating and how that sight changed him to a female. He told of campfires and cooking, of pudenda and bleeding, of a willingness for weeping and the hollow ring of boys' boasting. He told of seven years of thinking one way, while bodying another. And then in the same thicket of woods he chanced upon the same snakes, plying their trade once more. And then he told of the wager between King Friday and his stool wives, how he decided in favor of Friday on the issue of sex and gender, how the stool wives had poked out his eyes, how Friday had compensated him with drugs and dreams, and how he still hoped to live a normal life in a useful way.

"What do you make of this recitative?" Kimbene asked his tribe.

"The snakes are compelling," Ngugi said. "They are so apathetically unerotic that they are compelling. I believe him."

"The respent serpent repents the present," Lon Nol Lumumba said, using anagrams in a way that both amazed and annulled his king.

"He is lying," Brother Jero said, "like a, well a, as a snake in the kudzu."

"I wonder what Caruso would say," Stella said.

84

"I will tell you what he said," Tyree said, turning his head slightly askance and upward in the manner of certain blind soul singers. "La vipera che morisco a la suecera mori avellinata."

"He said this?" Stella asked.

"Verbatim," the boy answered.

"What does it mean?" she asked.

"I don't know," the boy said. "He didn't translate."

"Did he say this before the fire or after?" Kimbene asked.

"After."

Kimbene thought that he had trapped the boy with his trick question.

"Aha, and how did you know there was a fire, sightless boy?"

"I could smell the char on those who returned. It came in varying degrees."

"And did anyone perish in the fire?"

"No. They spoke of it as a minor pyre, a diminutive ignition, a little flashlight of a fire."

Kimbene knew instinctively that the boy spoke the truth and was not indulging in negative bragging. His inquisition with Naomi had prepared him well for the worst of news.

"I thought you might be one of the sole survivors. If you are not, then why are you here?"

"Silly me," the boy said, laughing and swatting his face at the same time. "I have almost forgotten my purpose."

He pulled an envelope from his backpack and handed it in the general direction of Kimbene.

85

"What is this?" Kimbene asked angrily. "There is nothing on this paper."

"The message comes inside, fully clothed," the boy said.

Kimbene opened the envelope and unfolded the paper. There were words in uniform rows, but this was not writing as he knew it.

"What is this, Ngugimahn?"

"This is called typewriting," Ngugi said. "A machine does what man cannot. It writes in perfect rows and even spaces."

"Do the Edo possess such a trick?"

"No, but now they do. This comes from Caruso's machine."

"How do you know this?"

"Because the writing is in italics."

"Read this thing to me."

" 'Dear Kimbene: Thanking you for your silent speech. Yes, we too are exceedingly fine. We have known about your baobab tree for quite some time. We are that tall. But we rejoice that you are growing, because it means we may one day see eye to eye. By that time we trust that you will be our subjects. I have need of someone to shine my Western shoes and you, Kimbene, may well apply for this position. As you can easily see, we have bypassed the written word, and soon this typewriting will go the way of the safari. We have already ordered our PC from Lagos. It is an AT&T 6600, with discs in both the erect and floppy states. The Italian you sent me knows something about boots, and with the minimum torturing I have convinced him to show me how to boot up. Maybe I will teach it to you too, if you come to potlatch at our place, which I have named Edo Congo. Don't bother asking for directions. We will come for you. With machetes and ropes. Sincerely, Friday. P.S. Kimbene, this is Caruso. Save me. I am being held prisoner. The Edo have much more food than you, but they are barbarians. I spend my days in a cooking pot. They light the fire underneath me, then pretend to forget about me while they have a smoke. Just before the water boils, they lift me out on a rope. I think they mean to eat me when the near-boiling joke has lost its novelty. Forget about a trade for me. They sent the blind boy because he is of no use to them.' "

Tyree had tears in his milky eyes. Ngugi sighed. The whole tribe was depressed.

"You will notice he said nothing about our fire," Kimbene said, grasping for any advantage he could.

"Indirectly he did," Ngugi said. "The torture of Caruso was probably inspired by our fire."

"What are we to make of this?"

"He sent Tyree instead of Caruso and succeeded in confusing us. Then he also sent this typewriting, the likes of which we have only seen in books from foreign presses, and he has once again succeeded in making us admire him."

"These Edo have learned how to fight very skillfully."

"I would say so," Ngugi said.

"I am so full of admiration I am tired," Kimbene

said. "Once again I must sleep on this problem. Naomi, will you assist me in my cogitation?"

"I have a headache," she said.

"Okay, then. You stay with the blind boy. We must find a way to give him back his sight. Ngugi, will you read me a bedtime story?"

"Of course, my liege."

"Bring to me *Anansi and the Spider* stories. We will yet prevail."

Inside the royal tent Kimbene was experiencing a crisis of confidence.

"This Friday is not Yoruba or Hausa. He is merely Edo, and yet he laps me with tricks of technology."

"This is so."

"But, Ngugimahn, whatever happened to the cult of personality?"

"It may be dying as we speak."

"Then the true and real kings may be dying as well."

"Sadly, this is so."

They continued to speak in this way throughout the night, for this was indeed the nadir of Kimbene's rural kingship. To continue to record such a conversation would entail an eavesdrop in dignity and risk a sentimentality of a sort such narratives are morally obliged to skirt. So perhaps a brief digression is in order, especially since certain essential facts have not been given.

For example, much of the terrain of this northeastern corner of Nigeria is comprised of grass savannas, which are alternately slippery and arid.

Lake Chad, in the extreme Northeast, is the only large lake in Nigeria. The climate here is typically tropical and parched, with temperatures rising to one hundred-fifteen degrees Fahrenheit. The trees of the region, in addition to the sacred baobab trees, are mostly hardwoods: oil palm, wild rubber plant, mahogany and ebony. In this section of the country locust, shea and tamarind trees also abound, as well as assorted acacia and mimosa trees. The population of the country approaches ninety million. The major cities are Lagos, Ibadan, Ogbomosho and Port Harcourt. The major exports are cocoa, peanuts, cotton, palm oil, soap and tin. The unit of currency is the naira, consisting of one hundred kobo per naira. In 1970 there were roughly 1,500,000 radios to 75,000 televisions, so sound beat sight by a twenty to one margin. By the turn of the century it is predicted that this ratio will have been reversed, although outlets and adaptor plugs remain a major obstacle. The major tropical diseases continue to be yaws, leprosy, sleeping sickness and malaria. Leprosy and malaria are treated seriously, while yaws and sleeping sickness are dealt with more poetically. Richard Lemon Lander (1804–34), although short-lived, was the first British explorer to set up a sphere of influence in Nigeria, and, although the British outlawed the slave trade during their colonial rule, the various tribes in Nigeria continued to practice the trade, as well as indulging in ancestor-worship, religious blood-feuding and other practices deemed "barbaric." With independence in 1960 Nigeria became a Federation with a supreme military council government, but with each region self-governing according to tribal customs. Thus, Nigeria is not unlike Paraguay in these and other respects.

Suddenly, it was morning and Kimbene called his tribe to a counting.

"These are my reasons," he began, "moving from the specific to the general, since that is what I am in this army. First, the hostage question. We mean this blind boy no harm. In fact, I rather like him. He tells great stories, and if he wishes, he could be my second fool, next to Perrymahn. Before we send him back, if he wishes to go back, we will have him fitted for eyeglasses. Thus, we will give him secondary sight. If the Red Cross ever returns, and if they bring with them the cataract mahn, we could then see if the light has indeed gone out in those eyes or if it is merely sleeping, as, I am told, polar bears in colder climes are wont to do. So. He is not a hostage. The Ibo do not take hostages. Slaves, yes, but not hostages.

"This leaves us with the other hostage. We did not ask Caruso to come here, and, although my stool wives like him personally, we cannot take responsibility for him. It is true we sent him to the Edo, but we did not force them to keep him. We gave him a chance to die honorably when we set the fire. We did not force him to save himself, thereby exposing himself to boiling cauldron humor among the Edo. We would like to avoid his martyrdom, because that might bring the emissaries of the Pope to investigate, but, short of that contingency, let us be plain about the tally-talker. He is no Kapuscinski. He is Caruso. Every man is a desert and no man is an island. Caruso knows that. Friday knows that. We can do nothing more on his account.

"This brings me to the central problem. The Edo have confused us with this blind boy. Then they have made us admire them with typewriting and threats of more. Ngugi assures me that the Edo have no outlets for a computer, so the Edo have bought themselves an expensive machine that won't work. Thus, the Edo have escalated their taunts to a point where nothing works.

"The trick to winning this war, it seems to me, is to reverse the polarities. We shall overwhelm them with our emissary and underwhelm them with our message. Where they have caused confusion in us by sending the blind boy instead of Caruso, we shall cause admiration in them by sending our most infirm, the leper Leopold. And, whereas they have caused us to admire them with their type-writing, we shall cause confusion in them by the understatement of our message. This, then, is the message I am sending back to them.

" 'Friday: I am in receipt of your rough draft. I must say you write a fair to meddling prose. We tire of this dalliance with you, for we still have much feasting to accomplish. And, since our boundaries are in question, we have decided to poison all the food in that proximity, the radius of which I must ruefully keep secret from you. For there to be struggle there must first be ambiguity, and we no longer feel ambiguous. We are certain that you have nothing to offer us. Keep Caruso. Keep our leper as well. Cook them and eat meat with our blessings. Kimbene.'

"These are my reasons. These are my decisions."

"We are starving to death," Brother Jero said. "What can you hope to accomplish by poisoning our boundaries with the Edo?"

"We don't need to do the deed. We merely need to intend to. And even if we did, how does one kill a dead crop?"

"This smells of logic," Ngugi said.

"But why threaten them with non-events?" Brother Jero asked.

"Time will tell you, not I," Kimbene said. "Now let us partake of an imaginary meal."

"Where is Leopold?" Bob Lumumba asked.

"I have already sent him," Kimbene said. "He ate early."

Then Kimbene showed them how to eat invisible food. With much gesturing of the arms, raising of the elbows, slurping at the mouth, the food was found to be quite good, even varied, as Ibo kitchens go. Little Tyree was simply amazed at how much he could eat without feeling full. Lon Nol Lumumba stuck his finger down his throat and indeed produced an upheaval of a concrete sort, proving to one and all that something had to have gone down for there to be this upcoming. Stella the stool wife, who had grown up in the darkness around campfires fighting for goat ribs and chicken wings flung carelessly by the elder men, was now apparently sated, for she refused a third helping.

Three days later, amidst rumors of little cannibalisms—people eating their big toe or thumbs—the sentries came back to camp with Leopold the leper and Caruso in tow. They also carried heaps of food: slabs of goat, pots of cassava, mango, pineapple, banana cream pies. The next day, there was more food. The next day, still more.

"What means this miracle?" Brother Jero asked.

"It means this," Kimbene said. "A people willing to poison their food are a people not to be beaten in war or else a people with such an abundance of food that they do not care. Leopold put the fear of leprosy among the Edo, and they were not able to think properly. They are humiliated. They send this food, thinking that we have no need of it, and thus are under no obligation to accept it. They will send still more."

"Shouldn't we, then, establish a peace between our peoples?"

"There is no hurry, Brother Jero. We will store the surplus food, while we get our own crops growing again. We win more by not declaring a peace. We can forget about the Edo now."

Everyone in the tribe was happy, except little Tyree, who decided he wished to return to his people.

"Even with devils we prefer the ones we are used to," Kimbene said.

"Egad. An adage," Perry Lumumba said.

"Have you learned anything from us?" Ngugi

asked the blind boy, who was now wearing wire-rim glasses.

"Lessons I shall never forget," he said.

They all said goodbye to the blind boy of the Edo and prepared for feasting. Even Caruso was ecstatic to be back among the Ibo.

"You canna know how famous I willa be. A prisoner of war, that is molto bene. I willa have a book, for sure."

"How did you survive your ordeal, then?" Kimbene asked, noticing that Caruso looked pink and bloated, quite soggy of skin and water-logged for those parched climates.

"The women," he said, winking at Stella and Della, "they throw bitsa root in the boiling kettle, something like a tuber, like our papas. They calla this thing cassava."

And he keeled over dead, before they could explain to him that cassava was poisonous until boiled and then beaten. He died thinking the Edo women had been kind to him, when they were merely being practical, throwing cassava into the pot he inhabited.

And so it came to pass that in the war between the Ibo and the Edo the only known casualty was an Italian journalist. True to his word, Kimbene did not count him.

IX

Famine is the female name for Africa. Hunger, beyond the bloating of a single belly, stretches to epidemic proportions. Food is as rare as a stopped rabbit in a tropical rainforest that teems with birds and snakes, the aliveness of such places a mockery of the fact that there is no food to sustain them. So, famine attaches to the female, even as birthing, stooling, cooking, grieving. It has to do with the time of their flow, the fact of their flow, the cycles of blood that are also mockeries, reminders of eggs not kept, death preceding life. It could not be otherwise, that in a tribal clan, a country, a continent, where fertility is the yardstick of all life's purpose, famine is the cradle song, the lullaby of lack, the hollow aftermath of each excess.

The women carry this shame of the species like a bone in the nose of a Bantu priestess or the serrated scars of knifecuts on the cheeks of prostitutes in the cities or the long lips like an idle ear on the vulva of women who have no memory of what virginity was or is or ever will be again. The terrain assumes it, the climate demands it, the grass savannas seem to will it, this shame of a violation without vulnerability, a violation upon the elders of one's elders, never experienced nor explained, from which there is no escape but to breed, be brown and brood, be silent and pass blood, as though the whole tribe were watching.

Men expel this sense of shame. They will not carry the burden of famine. In fact, they will do anything but look at it. It is not their crime if what they hunt is not there in abundance, if what they grow is swept away by monsoon flood, eaten up by ants and locusts, dried to voodoo shrivel by a drought. It is not their crime if what they see before them are women who please them, torture them, make them have to penetrate. They see no violation. A man who spoke excellent English was asked by a missionary to define illiteracy, and the man answered: "a man who has no offspring."

Men can go a long time without eating. Like a fast, without the mental purpose of a fast. They do not see scarcity as the lack of something that should be there, but rather as a clarity, a crispness caused by shrinking sight, a candor that feels natural, because the body is sloughing off itself. So, men can endure a long while of fasting. They grow fat from it. Their chests drop to their bowels, their eyes bulge, their ribs stick out like rungs on a ladder. Their knees bend and harden, like baseballs stuck on top of sticks. A dullness sets in. They linger. They no longer hide from the heat of the sun. Finally, their eyes unblinking, they are sullen with sleep, soft and brittle like a spider, and they do not even know they are dying when they die.

In women the famine is more physical. Their eyes are languid with lack of focus. Laughter sticks in their throats and they forget to feel. They forget to feel their children when they cannot feed them. They go inside their own bodies as into the deafness of a tunnel into which the screaming of children sounds like the false trill of faraway birds. The women sit or stand as long as they can, because they know instinctively that if they lie down they are lost. Their breasts droop to their stomachs, showing jags of scars, the nipples pointing downward like dowser rods. Their bellies swell and drop, hiding the genitalia. Finally, they stop producing eggs and cease to flow.

From early childhood they have been taught that they are like rivers, and then one day they cease to flow. They become scaffolding. Ebony, mahogany, the hardwood trees seem more alive. Their shame finally makes itself visible. In famine their shame is driven to the surface of their skin, where it shows itself as the caked slime that covers a stagnant pool.

They keep this look on their corpses.

X

When honey comes down from the mountains, lava erupts from the ground. This is an old adage, as old as dogs and fleas. Nobody knows the author.

The rural king Kimbene was getting tired of a rather ruthless agrarian economy when Ngugi came to him with two white men.

"Black blood spouts from the earth. It covers all our crops."

"Our ancestors spoke of just such an apocalypse," Kimbene said. "So, we are ruined. The soil has been spoiled."

"Wrong," Ngugi said. "You say the right word and don't even know it."

"I have no patience for these guessing games of yours."

"The black blood is oil," Ngugi said. "We shall be rich beyond all our wildest itches."

"And who are these white turds you stand between? You look like dominoes."

Ngugi moved away with his king, out of listening distance of the two white men.

"They are called Trevor and Fairfax. They come for the oil."

"How did they know it was there before me?"

"They have a nose for such things. They go around the world with their noses for oil. Trevor says he is American, but he speaks with a British accent. Fairfax says he is an American, but I have never heard English such as his. They represent oil companies. Trevor comes from Standard and Poors. Fairfax comes from Richland and Norm. They say they are world-wide and have many plastic cards to prove it. They come with dollars and promises. They are prepared for a bidding war."

"Will many be killed?"

"No, my king. They fight each other, to see who can give you the most money."

"I like these combats," Kimbene said. "Let them bid-fight, then. When we have reached the top of their dollars, we will declare the war to be a draw and let them both have our oil. Have we enough for both?"

"Oh yes, my king."

"Then let me grease the pig."

"Yes, my lord."

Kimbene took stock of the two strangers. Trevor was dressed in a sleeveless sweater and knickerbockers, and he puffed on a pipe. His demeanor, dignified. His tobacco, aromatic. He had crow's feet around his eyes, smile lines around his thin lips, brown spots on his delicate hands. Fairfax was, of course, the opposite. He was round and balding, ruddy-faced and damp with sweat. Standing still, he looked out of breath. He wore an orange pineapple shirt that deepened in color with sweat stains, so that it was terra-cotta in the tropics. He wore khaki shorts. The gold buckle on his belt was bold enough to blind anyone, even on a cloudy day. They both looked off-the-shelf and out-of-place, each one exaggerating the misfitting of the other.

"Oil men, I will interview you one by one. First, let me address the one who makes clouds when there are none in the sky. You are called Trevor?"

"That's correct, old boy."

"I am called Kimbene."

"Enchanté, I dare say."

"You have an English chip on your tongue, if not on your shoulder. Where do you hail?"

"I'm lapsed, as far as hailing goes. But I come from Sussex. No, Leeds."

"This is what Sherlock Holmes always said," Ngugi answered.

"Well, yes," Trevor said, stammering slightly in between puffs on the pipe. "That's in upstate New York."

"And why do you wish our oil?"

"For profit, of course. You know about that, do you?"

"We know about loss. But we can entertain the notion of profit as well."

Suddenly, there was nothing to say between them. Kimbene continued to stare, Trevor continued to puff, and time seemed to shift slightly, from one foot to the other.

"And you are called Fairfax?"

"Rightee, good buddy."

"I am called Kimbene."

"I know."

"Where do you hail, Fairfax?"

"I'm a good ole boy from Lubbock, Kim, if I can call you that. And I brung you a whole bagload a goodies for your palate there, Kim. You just feast your eyes on this spread: they's cornbread, candied yams, fatback, hamhocks, few pork bellies, pig knucks, black-eyed peas, collard greens, we call 'em corraled where I come from. You're sure enough a tall boy, but you got you some room to go horizontal-like."

"We are used to kola nuts as bribes," Kimbene said.

"Well, Jesus Jenny, if I'd only known. We ship you a case or two a Coca-Cola and some beer nuts big as gonads, no sweat."

"Why are you not oil-making with OPEC nations?"

"We do that too, Kim," Fairfax said. "We got more drills than all the dentists in China, if I can boast."

"We are used to boasting."

"Well, okay, then. Last Saturday week, I caught me a speckled perch, was biggern the whale what et ole Jonah. You buy that one?"

"I have my own theories about OPEC," Kimbene said. "Iran and Iraq, they are both oilers, yes? And what separates them?"

"I'd have to guess on that one, Kim, but I'd say an Ayatold you so or two."

"Their last letters only. N and Q. And what letters come between those two?"

"O and P," Trevor said, beating his rival to the answer.

"There you are," Kimbene said. "O and P. OPEC. So, Fairfax, let me quiz you more personally. I am thinking of growing a beard. What say you?"

"Shoot, Kim, where I come from, a beard's mostly good for hiding a coward's chin. We had a politico a while back, Barry Goldwater, he said having a beard was like having a third armpit."

"I like this answer," Kimbene said. "Let us drink in the trough of your golden waterberry."

"He'd like that, I'm sure."

"I am satisfied with both of you," Kimbene said. "Let us sleep on our respective capitalisms. In the morning you may begin your biddings."

"Will you accept traveler's cheques?" Trevor asked.

Kimbene didn't answer him. It was like music. One never answers a question after a coda.

He would have accepted ten dollars apiece, but they began the bidding at ten thousand dollars. After a year Kimbene was more than a millionaire. The Ibo ceased to grow their own food, make their own clothes, find and shape their own weapons. The art of ebony mask-making died out. There were

103

six wells upon their land, and the giant derricks cranked crude day and night.

At the Oil Barons' Ball, Stella the stool wife showed up in blue taffeta, even though the weather forecast was more or less predictably pluvial.

"My, but don't you look like Minnie Pearl, Missie Stella," Fairfax said.

"Spot of tea?" Trevor said, asking Della, who never refused anything narcotic.

"How do you like them oilers?" Kimbene asked Perry Lumumba.

"O.E.D. or rodeo?" the fool asked socratically.

"Yes, Perrymahn, they do rather run the gamut, don't they?"

Kimbene was not even aware of the contagion in his conversation, the alternating Alamospeak and nasal twang with dipthongs and mincing and other affected orations. He said "panacea" for full belly, "perpetrate" for any act beyond breathing, and "hot to trot" for any show of animal enthusiasm. He had gotten so leisured that he had begun using paper money, no matter the number of zeros, to start the evening fires instead of logs. He bought a bed for sexing his stool wives, into which he could put quarters for varying degrees of shimmy. He had thirty-seven pairs of Italian shoes, all with tapered toes, none comfortable enough for daily wear. Perusing the mail-order catalogues had replaced the afternoon siesta in the social order.

Trevor and Fairfax had finally convinced him not to stockpile his money, because he might lose everything in a forest fire or flood. They persuaded him to establish a portfolio and diversify: Swiss francs in Swiss banks, gold bullion, laser surgery stocks, fine art, failing utility stocks, real estate in Australia. At long last he had a portfolio the size of a metropolitan phone book.

One night Kimbene found Trevor sitting in a summer lounge chair out on the savannas underneath the plenitude of stars, of which, the Africans believe, there are as many as there are countries in the world. Trevor was puffing on his pipe, but he had no tobacco, and so he made no smoke. Unlike Fairfax, who sexed many women in the tribe, Trevor was a loner, something the Ibo fear and admire.

"So, Trevor, why do you perpetrate this chess of yours?"

"I like to lose at something."

"Is there not panacea in you?"

"More like a melancholy, I'm afraid."

"Do you miss Leeds this much?"

"Not at all. I'm giving myself over to the savage beauty of that sky."

"This is surrender of a silly sort."

"Perhaps. Why aren't you feasting, Kimbene?"

"I am not so hot to trot these nights. Maybe I have a melon in my collie too."

"You're a strange one, Kimbene. Aren't you happy to be rich?"

"Can one be both? I was happy before, when we made war on the Edo and had nothing to eat. Now that I am rich, I can't remember being happy."

"I suspect you're onto something profound there."

"I have noticed that you and Fairfax seldom commune. Black people are always together. Not you whites. Why is this?"

"We don't have a lot in common."

"You have the same skin color."

"That's not enough for white people, Kimbene."

"You have the oil."

"That drives us apart."

"You are both rich."

"Only relatively speaking. My company is rich, Kimbene, not me. I'm only their man on the scene."

"Then why do you work for them who never come to get the oil themselves?"

"I was just sitting here wondering that very thing."

"I will leave you, then, to lose at your chess and wonder such things. You do not make me laugh, Trevor, but I like you anyway. You have a home among the Ibo for as long as you wish."

XI

Kimbene knew this much about the nature of things: an image is more like any other image than it is like the thing it represents. He knew that real things had become as scarce as albino elders, replaced by simulacra, which increased and multiplied like biblical toads. For every motion, an emotion. For every sense, an absence. For every *res*, a *publica.* He knew that civilization operated biologically like a cancer, which would come to his tribe now that there was oil.

"Drat oil," Perry Lumumba said, and before he could finish his palindrome, Kimbene interrupted him.

"Yes, fool, I forgive your feminine rhyme. Indeed, the shells have come to look like peanuts."

So it was not entirely unexpected, given the nonchalant clairvoyance of the king and the oil-bearing affluence of the times, that other commerce should come looking for new markets, cheap labor and obvious tax advantages, and among them a group of Japanese image-makers, wishing to build a camera factory.

"I represent Nikon, Minolta and Mamiya, in that order," said Hibachi, the leader of the group.

In his entourage were twenty men, all in black suits, white shirts, thin ties. All were bespectacled, and they bowed their heads whenever Hibachi spoke, a sign of power, wealth and group discipline. Also in their entourage was one young woman, named Keiko, who was dressed in traditional kimono and obi sash. She was never formally introduced, and because of that fact, Kimbene deduced that she was the daughter of Hibachi.

Hibachi snapped his fingers, and several of his men produced squat bonsai trees, which they proceeded to plant at various asymmetrical distances, one from another.

"Apparently," Ngugi whispered into Kimbene's ear, "they have been to Israel."

The contrast was striking: all the short Asians surrounded by all the tall Africans. Some of the women of the tribe had never seen such jet-black hair, and they began to inspect their visitors for head lice.

"Elastin—nit sale," Perry Lumumba said.

"Anatono namaewa, nan desu ka?" Hibachi said, pointing a finger at Perry.

"He is my fool," Kimbene said. "I should tell you, Japan mahn, that we are not so hot to trot for simulacra like image boxes."

Hibachi smiled knowingly and produced a wad of yen from his pocket.

"Yen rot tami. I'm attorney," Perry said.

This offended the visitors, as did any mention of rot, but Kimbene suspected that Perry had merely elided rattan and tatami and that he merely wished to maintain some facsimile of legal advice during the transactions.

"Ask them what the former name of Japan was," Ngugi said.

"Pray tell," Kimbene said, "what was your land erst?"

"Edo," Hibachi said.

"Just as I feared," Ngugi said.

Of course, the Japanese had no way of knowing that their former name was the same as the present enemies of the Ibo.

"Edo malaria," Perry said, "air a la mode."

At this obvious slur Hibachi winced, bowing his head briefly and fiercely.

"This is not going well," Kimbene said. "We must find a common ground to strike an alliance. Something which transcends lucre, of which we have quite a lot."

"Wakarimasen," Hibachi said, squinting his eyes and scratching his chin in a posed sort of way.

"Ibo obi," Perry said, jumping for joy and pointing to Keiko, who tried to make herself invisible by blushing.

Hibachi had already drawn a dagger of the seppuku sort.

Kimbene understood what Perry meant. If Keiko

109

became the stool wife of the king, the business would go well.

"What say you, Ngugimahn?"

"An outrageous thought," he said.

But Perry Lumumba was not to be denied.

"Tie bra—arbeit," he said.

"My fool has used Nazi slanguage," Kimbene said, "but his meaning is sound. Tie bra, if indeed there is one, to sounder economic practice: that is, wed woman to work. If your daughter becomes my stool wife, you can build your factory and produce as many images as you please."

Hibachi looked overcast, like rain. His twenty men had all assumed defensive postures, which the Africans took to be flattering mimes, but which Ngugi understood to be various stances of karate, kung fu, t'ai chi and haiku.

"Would the tree ever know about swimming," Hibachi said, "if the branch had not fallen and floated down the river?"

"What is this enigma?" Kimbene asked.

"It is called koan," Hibachi said.

"I told you they've been to Israel," Ngugi whispered again in Kimbene's ear.

Then Hibachi produced the sound of one hand clapping and the deal was done.

Kimbene ordered a feasting, and he was surprised that such short people should be heavy feasters. By night's end Hibachi and his twenty men had all taken turns micturating on the campfire, boasting and toasting, and otherwise proving their manhood, their collective ginseng. Many of the men took pictures of the naked women in the tribe, using strobe lights, flash bulbs, tripods and even time-lapse photography. Kimbene noted how myopic his guests were, because all their pictures were of breasts, vaginas and buttocks, all in extreme close-up. Nothing was hurried or casual or spontaneous with them. They focused and refocused, their Seiko watches glistening in the reflection of the fire, rotating their voyeurism to a delicate science, the way archaeologists fondle a fossil. Eyes looked through spectacles which looked through lenses, prompting Kimbene to think of sexing as glass, which sexing could only climax in a shattering.

In the morning Kimbene challenged Hibachi to a game of one-on-one in basketball. The Japanese proved to be an expert dribbler, but Kimbene won easily with repeated slam-dunking. Hibachi was able to recuperate some of his face by beating Trevor at chess and Fairfax at arm-wrestling.

The next day Hibachi bid sayonara to one and all among the Ibo. His twenty men, all engineers and architects, stayed on, as did the new stool wife Keiko.

"Daughter," Hibachi said in parting, "of course I must disown you for this impure marriage, but I commend you for the enormity of the deal we have done here. You know your duty, your *on*, your *giri*, girl. Sit on this heathen's stool the way the bunraku sits on a hand."

"Domo, father," she said.

Kimbene admired the docility of the maiden,

who still wore her obi double-knotted, tighter than a fist. Of course, she refused all his sexual advances at first, even though Stella and Della and Naomi told her of his prowess at probing with the one-eyed fetish stick. But when he accused her of disobedience, he caught her unawares culturally, and she submitted to him, first with a silent scream, then with a confused mixture of shame and pretense, and finally with a banshee abandon, full of throating and moaning, the likes of hacksaws and hyenas, full of fingers digging, teeth biting, legs locking, and every other nook and cranny-sweeping, including obi-noosing his royal hardness until he said "Ohio" and she said "Toledo" and they both said "gozaimasu" and then they slept like puppies with their chins down and their ears drawn over their faces.

XII

The white man. He comes alone or in pairs. He comes two by two or in twenties. He comes with the fascination of the child for all wild things, for Africa is like his last frontier, his darkest dream, his tale full of the new-found surrey, signifying nothing. He comes unaware of danger, racial prejudice, tropical diseases and his own inappropriateness. At first, he comes in all humility, wishing only to strike a fast friendship and be treated as an equal, but sooner or later he finds a way to betray his host, to trick the tribe and deceive himself. And, however he is gotten rid of, there is only one certitude: he will come again. A different face perhaps, a varied accent, another tale to tell, but he always returns, with the same wide-eyed wanderlust in his eyes, the same wish to take a bath in the primitive, the same ugly loss of innocence in his memory, the same superiority complex.

113

Prosperity wore several hats in those brief halcyon salad days among the Ibo. Kimbene was still called rural king, but there was nothing much rural going on. The oil flowed freely and brought in wealth beyond counting. The camera factory was an enormous success. Nigeria was fast becoming noted for its candor, crisp focus and *cinema vérité* shots in *National Geographic, Paris Match* and *Der Spiegel.* There was a Seven-Eleven, run by Muslims from Lake Chad and occasional Pakistani refugees. There was a Fluffy-Wash laundromat. Signs of abridgment and civilization everywhere.

Could religion be far behind?

First came the Peace Corps workers, to dig sewers, install toilets and sanitary plumbing, pave streets. But the per capita income of this oil-producing tribe was so high that they had to be reassigned, and so they went off to Surinam or Mauritania.

Then came the Mormons, Tom and Amon, always in twos, in white shirts and smiling, with tales of Laman and Laban. They had absolutely no vices, except their missionary zeal. Kimbene wished them no harm, for they were both but teenage boys, but he saw no future for them in his tribe, and so one day he announced that Tom and Amon would be sexed by his stool wives Stella and Della as a tribal courtesy, and this was enough. Tom and Amon were gone the next morning.

Bishop Pike was another matter altogether. Even Trevor and Fairfax were sorely pressed to find any semblance of self-consciousness in this zealot. He came full of lurid stories of the lives of the saints, their many martyrdoms: Saint Peter, crucified upside-down; Saint John, boiled alive in a scalding cauldron; Saint Stephen, fleeced with arrows, even through the eyeballs; Saint Bartholomew, beheaded and eaten by cannibals; Saint Maria Goretti, stabbed forty-seven times by a sailor on liberty. The children were enthralled by such story-telling, and the women were drawn to the sheen of the zealot's eyes.

When Kimbene asked him to leave, Bishop Pike refused, and so Kimbene ordered Lon Nol Lumumba to hack off one of the prelate's hands. Bishop Pike blessed Lon Nol with his bleeding stump and said he had plenty of other cheeks to turn. So Kimbene ordered Lon Nol to hack off the other hand. Then one leg. Then the other leg. Bishop Pike was all bandages, but he was full of ecstasy at all these partial martyrdoms. In no way, shape or form was he going home, he said, and that was final.

At the evening feasting around the campfire, Kimbene thought he would have the better of the Bishop when all the men began to micturate upon the flames. Far from casting his eyes downward and feeling shame, Bishop Pike inched his way to the fire's edge, pulled himself up by a spinal spasm, and ejaculated several drops upon the fire. Then he looked to Lon Nol in a supplicating way.

"He wishes to be avowed and to aver," Lon Nol said, his machete raised.

"Then, asseverate him," Kimbene said.

115

And so the last extremity of Bishop Pike was hewn, and with the blow he expired, a look of frantic joy upon his face. Lon Nol, with the assistance of his brothers Idi and Bob, picked up what was left of the martyr and tossed him into the fire. In so doing, they scattered logs and embers, and all the tribe, even the new stool wife Keiko, felt a strange and serious contentment then, because they had helped this wretched man attain his goal.

"We must write this man, Neil Obstat. He is in all the church books. He will know how to include Pike with Bartholomew and Maria and all the others."

"Amen," Fairfax said.

"Nitro or tin," Perry Lumumba said.

And just when they thought they were blessed with secular wisdom, another godpot from America came, lured by the oil and the chance to put a pulpit in their midst. His name was Jimmy Biggart, and he was dressed in safari tan, beige and ecru.

He smote when he spoke, with spit and sweat and much prancing back and forth, working himself to a frenzy that Africans find banal and inane.

"I've come for your lean ones, yessuh, and your lepers too, praise Jee-sus, yessuh. I can feel him, name a Leopold, lordy me, ain't he scabby, though? I can heal him, lemme at him, I say. Bring me your poor and pitiful . . ."

He droned, he whined, he cavorted and shook, kicking up sand in a dance that nobody could follow. He scared the Japanese, who stayed home in

116

their bamboo houses. Everyone else knew why he was there. He had come for their money. He said money was the rack of the lamb, the root of all evil, the dog tooth that howled in the souls of men. He said he would take their bullion and barrels of oil, relieve them of all their temptation, take it all away on sacred ships, with ports of call in Babylon, Baal and other places, past and present, to be dispersed, scattered and sowed as the mustard seed at the eleventh hour, and nobody would be the wiser.

"Tuna nut," Perry Lumumba said.

"Man has, as it were, become a kind of prosthetic god," Ngugi said, noticing that the preacher showed a wooden leg when he hiked up. "Methinks Brother Biggart has been rejected by some other tribe."

"E lumber—reb mule," Perry said.

"Fool has a point there," Kimbene said. "With what he lacks in legs, he makes up for with stubbornness. I have no tact for such a man."

And he gave orders that Jimmy Biggart be bound and gagged. Then Lon Nol Lumumba shoved cockroaches into the nostrils of the preacherman, and the whole tribe watched him squirm and try to snort and sneeze them out. The cockroaches, for their part, wanted no truck with the preacher's proboscis, but the more they scurried, the deeper they became mired in his sinus secretions. Finally, Lon Nol extended his hands on either side of the preacher's nose, and with the full approval of his king he made a thunderous clap, smashing nose

117

and contents into a ground mush, which squirted out and dribbled down the distorted features onto the preacher's upper lip.

"Forgive us," Kimbene said, "for we know not what we do."

Then they bound his eyes and took the gagging off his mouth.

"We are going to sex you now with stool wives," Kimbene said.

Some of the tribesmen pushed the lips of a goat up to and against the preacher's lips. It has to be said that the goat was the first to pull away from such an embrace.

For a woman's breast they produced a kola nut, embedded in the flesh of an old mango that had lost its smell. The preacher protested, but then was seen to nibble with teeth and tongue until the mammary was taken away.

For the *coup de grace* Leopold the leper was ordered to proffer his buttocks to the preacher's face, but this conceit was short-lived when the leper let slip a petard, and immediately the preacher knew with what he was dealing. But Leopold was not through. He shook the man's hand, fondled his face, and pressed the open sores of his chest against the bare chest of the preacher. And then he whispered into Brother Biggart's ear.

"You are healed," he said.

Then they sent the preacher away in an ordinary car bound for Lagos. Whether the preacher ever contracted leprosy or not, Kimbene never knew. But he spoke at once to the whole tribe.

"Brothers and sisters, this may have been our last chance to save our souls, if indeed we have souls and if indeed they needed saving. So, let us hear no more of fire and brimming stones from the whites."

Having made his modest speech, he proposed a new round of feasting, and although everyone by now was tired of the gala, nobody refused him.

XIII

With notoriety came news, the two words being synonymous for the Ibo and neither one especially valued. But it came to pass that the tribe of the rural king Kimbene was invaded by the cameras and crew of *Sixty Minutes,* and Kimbene dismissed this invasion as he had dealt with the invasion of the neighboring Edo—as the narcissism of minor differences. He had never watched television, so he had no cultural context for being watched on television. As far as he was concerned, the interview they came to do with him was merely one more white hiatus in an otherwise black chain of being. He was neither nervous nor especially curious. Other things fell out of the sky. Why not an American camera crew?

"So, Kimbene, shall we begin? Let me say right off the bat that I'm a little intimidated by your

121

height. You are incredibly tall. How tall are you? Over seven feet?"

"Yes. Over."

"How much over?"

"It doesn't matter, once one is rural king."

"I see."

"I too see, Sawyer, that you are incredibly white. How white exactly?"

"Yes, well, blond."

"And I have noticed you have breasts."

"Thank you, yes. Two of them."

"Are you stool wife for Ed Bradley?"

"That's absurd. I don't know who your sources are . . ."

"Ngugi, who is wise in all things. My ancestors. Any water that flows in Nigeria. These are my sources. Which are your sources?"

"Yes, well, we don't divulge that sort of thing. Now about the oil."

"The black blood that ruins our crops."

"Yes, true, but it's made you incredibly rich. How can you maintain that you are still a rural king when your entire landscape has been transformed?"

"I am still rural king. We are oil farmers. That is all."

"You have a sense of humor, Kimbene. Every estimate indicates that you are richer than all other rural kings put together, that you are richer than all the regional kings put together, that you are richer, some say, than all the businesses in Lagos."

"But I have no money at all."

122

"Come now . . ."

"You may search our huts. Whatever you find you may keep. All the money is, how you say, invested? To me this means divested. They are same. No money. I have coral beads and kola nuts."

"Very astute. But aren't you afraid of reprisals?"

"What are these?"

"Attacks from your neighbors the Edo, who are envious? Perhaps being destooled by Achebe, your regional king? Perhaps assassination by the military regime in Lagos?"

"We have always been attacked by the Edo, Sawyer. We don't need oil for that. And nobody has ever seen Achebe. And I don't know anything about these people in Lagos. If they want oil from us, they come. We give it to them. If they want money, they come. We give them. We got plenty both for everybody. You want money, Sawyer?"

"Thanks, no, that's not the point."

"Why did you come here then?"

"For the story, of course."

"What story?"

"The rags-to-riches story. In Africa, surrounded by famine and hardship, your rural economy has become a booming oil economy. It's like the lottery back home. Americans like this kind of story."

"You mean, they like to watch?"

"There's a fascination. A pleasure. An envy. A resentment. And, yes, they like to watch. We like to watch."

"This is not to be confused with living?"

"You're splitting hairs with me, Kimbene."

123

"I don't know what this means, but I would like to split them, yes. You know what is fascination for me?"

"Tell us."

"That when we talk and all there is is talk, no descriptions, then the outside world is in a drought."

"Evaporates?"

"Yes, that, and hollows too. Like a tunnel."

"We might say a phone booth."

"Yes. And then soon the talking has no place to it."

"In other words, we could be in the K Mart parking lot?"

"I don't know, yes. And with no place, no body. No point of view. And then the talk becomes all voice, language instead of rivers and grass savannas, words instead of thatched huts and leather sandals, metaphors instead of machetes and cooking and smelling the food or even smelling each other. This is what I do not understand about television. It puts all the pictures into a box, and still they are not enough. So, there is this talking. All these words to hide the fact that the pictures have no corners."

"This is a very profound analysis of the medium. Rest assured, Kimbene, that there will be more to my report than these tight close-ups of you and me. There will be aerial shots of Lake Chad. There will be shots of women stamping the cassava. There will be shots of lions and monkeys. That's what we call editing."

"Then you will lose these faces of you and me."

"Not lost. Interspersed. Collaged. Given a certain rhythm."

"Lies."

"No, Kimbene. We do our best to report accurately. We're known for that. Tough questions. Tight close-ups. That certain *Sixty Minutes* cutting."

"Cutting is tricking, which we Ibo appreciate, but which is also lying."

"How so?"

"An example. We have temporality here. So, if when I wake in the morning and decide to wear shoes, there is only me and shoes. I look at shoes. Feel shoes. Smell shoes. Maybe I start with right foot or maybe with left. Then there are laces. I tie them. Maybe I sit with the feel of my feet in them before I stand. Maybe I change my mind and take them off again. There is nothing waiting, no after-my-shoes. No bus. No clock. No buying or selling. There is only the temporality of tying shoes, you see? And some days this might take in your counting ten minutes. Other days, this might take four hours, especially if I have drunk much palm wine and warm beer the night before. But you are impatient, yes? I have come to understand the whites think we live slow. We eat slow. We talk slow. We walk slow and sex slow and die slow. So by now you have already cut the shoes off my legs and replaced them with water buffalo eating grass or airplane-looking at Lake Chad. You are impatient, you have gotten tired of the truth, and so you lie

125

with water buffalo which are not me and can never fit on my feet and you lie with Lake Chad which is not here and cannot be here. And then your people who watch and do not live think these are all the same things: Kimbene, water buffalo, Lake Chad. But no shoes. No laces. No feel of the feet. No temporality. And I have been so slow to explain this that you will edit me too, this what I say, so that even the example of an example is cut and lost forever. Is this not so?"

"I'll do my best to keep it in, Kimbene, but I can't promise you. Can I ask you some tough questions now?"

"You can ask."

"I want to focus on the subservient role of the women."

"With your camera?"

"No. I was using 'focus' as a figure of speech. Let me put it to you this way. To be rural king, you have to be tall."

"The tallest."

"Exactly. So, this excludes women from ever being king."

"But they do not want to be king. They want to be stool wife."

"Exactly. But, then, there is no equality?"

"This is in the nature of being king. A king is not equal to his subjects. He is taller. That is why he is king."

"To repeat myself: exactly. There is sexism, then, in this exclusion."

"No, there is only exclusion. In the same way that

I am excluded from ever being short. This is tall-ism."

"But have you ever asked your stool wives if they wanted to be king?"

"Why would I ask? I know this answer."

"Well, I certainly wouldn't be happy with being just a stool wife."

"Has anyone asked you to be one?"

"Not in so many words, no. Let's move on. You resist monogamy, don't you?"

"No. But I admire fertility."

"And birth control? Has the government tried to enforce any birth control methods?"

"I am the government."

"I mean the one in Lagos."

"Why should they? They are Lagos, they are there. We are Ibo, we are here."

"Have you thought of doing any noble deeds with your wealth? Any honorable acts? Charitable concerns?"

"I feed Leopold, the leper. He does not starve."

"How about public works? Say, erecting buildings?"

"We have built some toilets. They are only partially successful."

"Do you miss the land, the farming, the way it was before?"

"Yes. I always miss the way it was before. This has nothing to do with oil and wealth. This has to do with reading and writing."

"Do you think you will come to America one day?"

127

"I would like this, yes, if I could do so without abdicating my stool and abandoning my people. I would like to eat in restaurants. I want to eat this blur food."

"You mean, fast food?"

"Yes."

"I'm told you love the game of basketball."

"Yes. I am good at slam-dunking."

"Are you familiar with some of our African players? Hakeem Olajawon?"

"The Dream. Former Twin Tower. Now single minaret, yes."

"And Manute Bol?"

"No. We do not know of him."

"If you came to America, what kind of souvenirs would you take back with you?"

"A white stool wife, of course. A potato, or other form of edible tubers. Some of your mini-machetes, the double ones that you call scissors. Fertilizer. Lawn-Boy products. Bubble gum. Otis Redding albums. Cowboy boots. These are some of your products I covet."

"An interesting list. You might visit and decide you'd like to stay."

"I don't think so. There is the memory of slaves there. And you have no kings, no respect for kings. I would miss that. And I would miss making war on the Edo."

"We're coming to the end of the interview. Do you have anything to say to Americans about the shape of the future?"

"The future always takes the shape of a woman.

It curves and bends and folds and sings you to sleep. We will not come to you, but you will come to us. Do not fear our tallness. Fear jihads. These are my pronouncements."

"Thank you, Kimbene. May you live long and prosper."

"May you also swell, Sawyer."

XIV

And then one day the oil, like every other liquid thing in Africa, dried up. What had been a geyser slowed to a trickle, and the trickle stopped to drops, black mud, earth caked with fissures, the stuff of chimney-sweeping. The black cranes came to a halt, like giants yawning, caught standing up with sleeping sickness. The women wept, the children tore out their hair, the warrior men began to look for their weapons, as though a price had to be paid. Fetish sticks were beaten freely. The sun hid behind black clouds that billowed and seemed bloated with oil.

The rural king Kimbene sought out Trevor and Fairfax for an assessment. He found the former out on the grass savannas, checkmating himself.

"Where is Fairfax?"

"I'm afraid, old boy, that his ship has sailed."

"Brother Jero reports his daughter Kampala among the missing."

"Hmm. Old Fairfax will have some explaining to do to the wife and kids in Lubbock. Perhaps he will say Kampala has come *au pair*."

"He did not say goodbye."

"I fear there are reasons why."

"Oiling days are over?"

"Yes."

"Will the cranes and derricks leave us too?"

"We generally leave them to rot a bit."

"Why?"

"Just in case. With oil you never know. We rob the graves and leave the markers."

"But we are still incredibly rich?"

"I think perhaps you trusted Fairfax too much on that score. I tried to tell you, but you wouldn't listen."

"Explain, Trevor."

"Not much to explain really. You haven't got a bird in the hand, so you haven't got two in the bush."

"My wealth is not in birds?"

"Sorry, old chap. I was easing the blow with a cliche. Those Swiss francs in Swiss banks? Fairfax has all the numbered accounts."

"My gold bullion?"

"More bull than bullion. Fairfax melted down all the real gold. Shipped it in barrels marked for crude."

"My failing utilities stocks?"

"Still failing, I suspect. You should hold onto them, just in case."

"My real estate in Australia?"

"Acres of quicksand or some such. You have been had all around."

"I should have invested in monarchies."

"Few of them left. They would have taken your money with them into exile."

"You stayed behind to tell me this? Are you not afraid that I will do to you what I would have done to Fairfax, had I known?"

"I thought of that. Guess I felt responsible. Do what you must."

"And if I let you go too?"

"My company has recalled me. I'm supposed to go to Paraguay. Some new oil fields there. It's a step down. A demotion, actually."

"So you will do this?"

"You mean I can leave with your blessing?"

"Yes."

"Can I also stay with your blessing?"

"I do not see . . ."

"I've got no family. After twenty-five years I've grown tired of the business. I don't fancy myself living off a pension in Leeds. Tea and scones. Bad soccer on the telly. I'm happy down here. I'd like to live out the string down here."

"You still do not make me laugh, Trevor. In fact, it makes me sad, every time I talk to you. But I will grant this wish of yours. You will be a reminder to me and the whole tribe of what fools we were."

"Thank you, Kimbene. I'm sorry about Fairfax."

"Forget about Fairfax. Kampala will one day make our revenge. She carries it in her blood."

With the end of the oil economy came the end to all other commerce as well. The laundromat closed. The Seven-Eleven closed. The Pakistanis went home. The Japanese went home. Within weeks the Ibo had a ghost town on their hands. The giant oil derricks, now derelict, were declared windmills. The children played hide-and-seek in them, and they became the favorite latrine of nomads and animals.

News travels fast in one direction only. Whereas the entire world seemed to know immediately about the oil boom, nobody but the immediate Ibo seemed to know about the bust. Ngugi informed Kimbene of rumors that the Edo were about to start another war, this time with the oil fields as the disputed prize. There were rumors of hit men hired by foreign powers to "waste" Kimbene and start an oil cartel. There were rumors of destoolment from a jealous regional king Achebe. There were rumors of a war of spanking and attrition, to be initiated by the military regime in Lagos, who had all of the uniforms, discipline and advanced weaponry, but none of the oil. There were also rumors of a more diplomatic war, by which the legislators in Lagos would win away the oil of the Ibo by way of income taxes, import and export tariffs, and personal property tax hikes. There were no rumors of good news.

During this same period the stool wives Stella

and Della gave birth to their second issue, this time both daughters whom Kimbene named Millie and Molly, after a favorite fanciful poem by e.e. cummings. When informed that the rage in Best Western countries for naming black daughters was the Africanization of names—Latoya, Lateefa, Kadeeja, Malika—Kimbene shrugged his shoulders like Sisyphus and said that had he gotten a son out of this second round of offspring, he would have named him Olaf, after another favorite e.e. cummings poem, and he stressed that he still held in high esteem the poetry of gwendolyn brooks, sonia sanchez, nikki giovanni, et al.

Kimbene began to refer to this temporality as "my time of drowning," even though drought prevailed everywhere. The grass savannas turned brown with neglect. Monkeys screeched from hunger in the forests. Wild animals came out of hiding and lay on their haunches, stupefied by the sun. The moon was like a pale mockery of the next day's blinding heat. The scorched earth constricted like a boa, hugging bare feet with a sticky paste that turned out to be human blood. Men forgot to micturate on the evening fire. A drought prevailed everywhere.

The first assassination attempt came in the guise of a traveling salesman, hawking coral beads, kola nuts, mandrake root, ginseng and M16 rifles. The latter caught the attention of the wise Ngugi, who asked the man in Edo dialect the price of a string of coral beads.

"If you have to ask, you can't afford it," the man said, before realizing that he had been flushed from a thicket like a fox by a hound.

Before they could subdue him, he had turned his M16 on the tribe. Three people died. Another eight were wounded. Lon Nol Lumumba snuck up on the man from behind and beheaded him with a machete.

The second assassination attempt came in the form of a postal courier from Lagos, whose mail pouch bulged suspiciously.

The courier said he had a Special Delivery letter for Kimbene, return receipt requested, which required the signature of the king. As he made his way through a gauntlet of Ibo to the waiting monarch, Idi Lumumba shot him with the M16 of the previous assassin. And, before Kimbene could chastise his subject for this giddy Gidean *acte gratuit*, the mailman, the mail pouch and all the explosive contents therein blew up, leaving three more dead and another eight wounded.

"When is the Red Cross going to come?" Kimbene wondered.

"We're still waiting," Ngugi said.

"Godot—to dog," Perry Lumumba said.

"Fool is right," Kimbene said. "In these strange days we can no longer tell men from beasts and beasts from gods."

"What is apocalypse backwards?" Bob Lumumba asked his brother.

"Mood," Perrymahn said.

The third assassination attempt came in the form

136

of a Muslim jihad, which struck by night, but was foiled, because Kimbene had ordered the last remaining barrels of oil to be spilled around each hut, and the terrorists slipped, got stuck or slid sideways, while sentries in the treetops and oil derricks took them out with bows and arrows.

"Maybe we should move," Ngugi said, surveying the pile of bodies to be burned by morning's light.

"They would still come," Kimbene said.

Then he got an idea, his inspiration coming from the signs the Pakistanis had put in the windows of the now-defunct Seven-Eleven. He ordered signs to be put up on the one road and all pathways leading into and out of the tribal lands. The signs said: WE HAVE NO MORE OIL. NO MORE THAN TWENTY DOLLARS IN TILL AT ANY TIME. SECURITY ALARMS BY POSITRON.

He hoped these signs would discourage future assassination attempts, although he knew they would only be effective if the would-be killers were literate. And, if they were literate, then they likely had achieved higher stations in life than hit men. Ngugi knew this too, and he brooded close to his boyhood friend.

They knew they could not discourage attacks by the Edo, for these were a fact of life. Neighbors are predisposed to kill each other. And they knew foreign oil companies would become weary of hiring jihad mercenaries when their annual reports verified the fact that there was no more oil. That left the threat from Lagos. They decided to deal with this threat by sending Trevor to Lagos to spread the word that all the oil had dried up. The military regime in Lagos would believe a white oilman, especially one with such sadness and lassitude as Trevor possessed.

"Yes, and maybe I will go with him."

"But, Kimbene," Ngugi said, "you, yourself, said that your enemies would only follow."

"Follow—wollof," Perry said.

"Mine enemies are not Senegalese, fool," Kimbene said. "Maybe they will ensue," he said to Ngugi, "but they will have ensued me alone and not my full tribe."

"Then you would ab . . .?"

"Dicate. Exactly. This is the problem. If I could only find some way of going for a week . . ."

"A fortnight," Trevor said.

". . . without my people knowing I have gone," Kimbene continued. "This would be no small trick. No mean ruse. I must sleep on this one."

He slept on the problem and nothing came to him. In the morning three more people were dead and another eight were wounded, but there had been no attack, no assassin, no bullets, knives, spears, bows, arrows, mortar, pestle.

"If my enemies have learned foreshadowing, then my cause is lost," Kimbene said.

The tribe fell to trembling, whining and every which way weirding. They had never dared to hope in the first place, but then panic has never been proven to be the opposite of hope either.

When into their midst a stranger strolled, a tall

stranger in western blue jeans, hands in his pockets, a hobo, himself depressed, needing a shave and assurance. And of course the warriors feared he was another hit man. Lon Nol Lumumba was ready to bash his head in with a boulder, when Kimbene waved him off and ordered the stranger frisked. Hands in the air, the hobo allowed himself to be fleeced, for there was nothing on his person or in his pockets. He said his name was Ajax, which was not a common African name, and this information gave rise to new suspicions, but the stranger was so tall that Kimbene was curious and spared him further insult. He ordered Brother Jero and the Board of Interviews, who also doubled as Chief Magistrate of Police and Deputies, to escort Ajax to the royal hut and there to stand guard with their bobbysticks, which were in truth fetish sticks.

Lon Nol was frantic.

"First, three people die and eight are wounded," he said. "Then the stranger comes. Next you will die as mysteriously and the stranger will leave, with temporality obscuring the evidence."

"Nay," Kimbene said.

"Why, pray tell, not?" Ngugi asked.

"The stranger is beautiful-tall," Kimbene said. "I have looked straight into his eyes, without bowing my head or lifting my chin, and, even though he be a tatterdemalion with an unlikely name, still he has stature."

"This is narcissism of the silly sort," Ngugi said.

"Then I will tell you more. Remember the lines?   *

And if the sun comes

How shall we greet him?

These lines came to me, to sandwich a vision I have
had, that of the sun shining around the contours of
the blank moon, red and orange and on fire around
the circle, with a big brown spot in the middle."

"The solar anus," Ngugi cried.

"The same," Kimbene said. "When this vagrant
came into view I saw the fires form a halo around
his head, and his face was in brown shadows."

"Then he is a god?" Lon Nol Lumumba asked.

"No, he is a bum," Kimbene said. "But he happens to coincide with a royal vision, and so he will
be spared the usual indignities and given sanctuary
in the king's quarters."

The tribe was temporarily convinced.

But Kimbene had something altogether different
in mind. He confronted Ajax in his hut.

"You should be a king somewhere, strange man.
Instead, you come to us in rags, smelling of rot and
wrestling. I am compelled to trust in you, if only
because you are shocking-tall. I have in mind a minor abdication of my kingship, for the purpose of
going off to Lagos. I shall be back within a week.
You have only to stay inside these quarters. You
may sit, stand or sleep, but you may not go outside.
My intimates will feed you well, better than anyone
else in the tribe. Not even my stool wives are to
know the difference between you and me. My people will not know if it is you or I inside. In this way
may I go freely, without abandoning my people,
which I would never do. If when I return you have

140

kept your bargain, you may indeed assassinate me, if that is your purpose. You are wondrous-tall and your height will spare you the wrath of the tribe. You will then be known as the rural king of these Ibo. And if you are someone else and have no thought to kill me, then you will be more than my guest. You will be my equal in every way, something I have never had. Is this bargain acceptable to you?"

Ajax nodded his head.

"Then partake of my life," Kimbene said, and he left under cover of night with Trevor for Lagos.

During Kimbene's absence only Ngugi was allowed inside the hut. He told the people that Kimbene had taken ill and needed rest and quiet. In this way did he stave off the stool wives and assure the tribe. But he, himself, was far from assured. Several times he tried to trick the stranger into revealing his purpose. He spoke to Ajax in Edo dialect, but Ajax did not answer. He aped Muslim prayer mantras, but Ajax did not respond. Only when he read Shakespeare to the tall stranger did Ajax seem to smile benignly and go to sleep.

When the real Kimbene emerged from his hut for the evening fire and round of toasting and boasting, there was great rejoicing all around. The tribe had quite forgotten about the murky stranger and cared only to see the face of their beloved king. The stool wives, stalled for a week's time, were lined up for sexing. Kimbene tried to dissuade them, thinking that he could not perform adequate acts in front of a stranger, but they would not be dissuaded. To his great surprise, Kimbene found when he went to his hut that the stranger had disappeared, apparently caring neither for assassination nor for kingly equality.

"An hautboy," Kimbene thought with some amusement, for his companion Trevor could not pronounce an H to save his life, and he referred to the hobo as oboe.

And sexing produces, not only partial forgettings, but whole oblivions, which is to say that after linking with four stool wives Kimbene, too, had quite erased the towerful stranger from his mind.

XV

Kimbene. The signature should always come before the message, just as the announced voice in
written theater, not end it. This is true for time sig-
natures as well. Eyes on the horizon. Hands to the
heart. I have committed myself to writing. I will
interview myself on the occasion of my trip to Lagos with Trevor, because no one else will ask the
questions.

Kimbene. I feel reborn each time I pen these particular letters. They are more than adjacent, like
suburbs to a city. They create me. Or perhaps they
begin my death.

In truth, this was not my first trip to Lagos. Uncle
took me there when I was twelve. He said he had
trading to do and wanted a companion. But I feared
he was taking me to leave me there, because I was
a tall boy, I ate much food, and Mother might
be getting desperate. Uncle had never shown me

any particular favor. Mother had never allowed me to go to the neighboring tribe, never mind Lagos. So, when Uncle said he would take me and she agreed, I became suspicious. I scattered bread crumbs for the first five kilometers, but then I ran out of crumbs and despaired of ever seeing Mother again. Uncle said nothing to me during the entire trip, but he *did* bring me back with him, for which I was most grateful, especially when I saw that my trail of crumbs had been erased by hungry birds.

Trevor told me once that writing and speaking were opposites. As chances would have it, those who do well in speaking are likely not to be good writers, and vice-versa. As an emerging writer, I do have theories of my own. I think writing is the per-version of two-person joy. When there is no true talking, words between two people, there is writ-ing. Yet this writing is kingly, savage, contrary, and, like Trevor, melancholy. It is like the hollow-ness after sexing, the mark of the stool wife still on my forehead, the memory holding, hanging on, trying desperately to fill the absence where we were, but finally losing. So that this loss may not be entirely silent, I write.

On the Naming of Certain Cities:

I went to Lagos, expecting to be treated like a king. Instead, I was ignored. I received stares in the streets for my height, but not for my kingship. Faceless eyes took notice and squinted, as though my size had distorted them. I was foreseeably tall, but still anonymous on those city streets. They had

144

no need of reverence for rural kings. I stood in line for stamps. I waited to be seated in restaurants. I smelled open gutters that no one else seemed to smell. The city takes people in, they mistake the lack of obstacles for a welcome, and they do not realize their mistake until it is too late to leave. The city is as impersonal as the lion's leap that fells the gazelle; as impersonal as the hairy husk of the coconut, hacked off a tree and stripped of its milk; as impersonal as both of these things, and twice as violent.

In Africa the large cities are the only places that are not green. We have so many shades of green: emerald green to Easter basket grass the missionaries first showed us; pea soup to Army green, which in Nigeria is more brown than green; verdant to bitter vetches; lime, slime and algae green; mint, coral and collard green. There are occasional yellows, shades of yellow for the animals and clusters of fruit like the plantain, which can also be green. And there are browns, all shades of brown and black and pink for the people who live here, but all these other colors must blend with green, except in the cities, which are rust-colored, dusty and dank, and which produce the only shades of gray on the continent.

And yet the roads lead to the cities. Farm land shrinks before our eyes, and the troubled future of all African peoples lies this way, crowding the already-crowded cities. In every city, the same sights: pollution beyond the means to cope with it; a marketplace stubbled with bodies and wakened by human sweat, where more people walk by than buy; small jails, overcrowded schools, an exhausted water supply; a few rich houses, to which the many aspire; spreading slums, in which youths run rampant and their parents sit outside on stoops and brood, emotionless, as though they were guarding a vault.

While we were walking the main streets of Lagos, a plane flew overhead, skimming the rooftops and making much din.

"A red cross," Trevor said, noting that marking on the plane. "Must be carrying the sick or infirm."

"Malaria—air a lam," I said.

I had decided in advance that I would speak as often as I could in palindromes, like Perrymahn, thinking I could, by remaining aloof, fool a countryman or two.

We were hungry much of the time. Trevor insisted we eat in one of the indoor sit-down restaurants instead of the more-frequent outdoor cafes. We waited in line for an interminable temporality, and finally I said, loud enough for the other patrons to hear, that I noticed the flies were having an easier time of getting a table than the humans. We were seated at once.

Trevor noticed much clamoring going on behind the walls, the sound of grunting attaching itself to the sound of moaning and irrational chatter. It sounded very much like sexing of an institutionalized sort. The sound was the harbinger of a visit to our table by an extremely tall and pastel-clad prostitute, her body the shape of an ocean wave standing upright, her hair thrown back in what is called a ponytail.

She looked at us strangely, the melancholy white man flanked by the exceedingly tall stranger.

"Do you want servicing?" she asked Trevor, with a British accent.

"No, my dear, not tonight."

She then offered me.

"Lagos. So, gal. Oda ado?"

I might as well have been a twin or occasional harelip. My palindromes were taken as a sign that either I was possessed or else I was a fool. She smiled politely and withdrew.

Trevor was impressed with my handling of the situation. My mind was already on the after-eating, the paying for the food.

The naming of cities is a serious occupation. If you want your cities to be flooded with people, then you will end your cities in -ville, -town or -burg. If you want your cities to seem sedate for settlement, you will give them women's names. Thus, Johannesburg is doubly flooded, while Timbuktu is underpeopled. In our newly-emerging countries, the tendency is toward African names. If these are hard to pronounce or spell for Best Western tourists, then they will not come, because, without having moved on the map, the places will seem more remote, more treacherous, less civilized. Certain consonants are deceptively alluring. For example, cities which begin with the letter L: Lagos, Lahore, Lisbon, La Paz. These are all water names and will attract many people. Conversely, cities that begin with vowels repel the capitalists: Akra, Entebbe, Ulan Bator, Ibadan, Islamabad. These names sound "native": to Best Western tourists they sound like towns full of thieves and murderers, and such tourists will not come to them.

The future census and sovereignty of all our developing nations will depend upon the judicious naming of new cities and the shrewd renaming of old cities, so as to confound the mapmakers, foreign merchants and mercenaries as well as the missionaries.

The Failure of Photography:
While I was in Lagos with Trevor, I asked him if he noticed anything of particularity.

"To what do you refer?" he asked.

"Refer?"

"Yes, it's a perfectly good English word, and I know you know the meaning."

"Trevor, you are palindroming," I said, smiling.

I repeated my question. He looked around, shrugged his shoulders, said there were the usual sights and sounds associated with any Third World city: nothing more, nothing less, everything in its chaotic place. What I noticed was that there were many true languages, but no true images.

If you ask a black man to recite a poem for you, he can do so. He puts his body behind the words, and the recitation becomes theater. The chances are strong that his poem has never been written down anywhere, for this is how we keep the language hot: rhyming and timing and alive like a kitchen. If you ask a white man to recite a poem, unless he

148

be a poet by trade, he will say: "Why?" or "Which one?" or "I don't know any." And, if by chance he knows one, it will be short: a limerick, haiku or Hallmarker. He will stand stiff and still as he recites. He will deny his body from the words, as though to keep his identity distinct from them.

While in Lagos, I heard an extraordinary kind of poetry called "the dozens." They sometimes had titles: "Stagger Lee," "The Sinking of the Titanic," "The Signifying Monkey." These were very long poems, full of toasting and boasting, with main characters named Simple or Slim, and they were always about sexing. I cannot tell you how distracting and delightful these poems were.

But, if white people now speak dead languages, they still own the images. Have you ever noticed how impossible it is to capture a black person accurately in a photograph? He is always overexposed, electrocuted, portrayed as burnt toast, so dark his eyes shine, his teeth shine, all his white places glow. Or if he is less singed with light, so that he appears a passable brown, then everything else in the photograph will be underexposed, half-colored, not its real self, and so not really there.

Our Japanese, before they went home, eschewed the color photograph, because there is no true yellow, and they came out looking blue or red. They preferred black-and-white photography, which of course made them look like white people.

The photographic process, then, is a white process. It was invented to portray accurately the absence of color.

This falsity of the image is not only true of photography. It is true of any depiction. In the post office in Lagos I saw drawings of wanted criminals. They were, I suppose, meant to be drawings of black people, based on hair style, roundness of eyes and lip size. But these faces had no blackness to them. Their foreheads were white, their cheeks were white, everything that was not a prominent feature was white. Who knows where to find these white black people?

I said to Trevor: "They will not be caught in my lifetime."

He thought I doubted the justice system. What I doubted was the justice of the image. Sometimes, they are the same.

On Cinemas:

While in Lagos, I went to many cinemas. I especially liked the matinees, because they put the night back into the day. I was much amazed by what I saw. Heads without bodies, hands without arms, food that looked and sounded like real food, but did not have a smell. Trevor told me that cinemas were a way to transcend illiteracy in Africa. People who couldn't afford to buy a book could afford cinemas, and in this way many novels were put to moving. I wanted to know who was doing the looking, but he said this was not important.

On Billboards:

Trevor said to me: "What goes around comes around."

This statement seemed to me not only the perfect

definition of a palindrome, but also of a billboard as well. Billboards are a form of weaponry. They pretend to be about words, but they are really about images, and these images persist in the brain, so that the eyes of the driver, still on the road ahead, do not even think they have seen the images. And billboards are like an attachment to the automobile. They look independent of the automobile, but they are really like a ventriloquism, an arm removed from the body.

There are no needs for billboards in an airplane or on a speeding train. Only the automobile attracts them. They are an occasionally welcome digression from a hot and monotonous road, but how is this so? It is because they are flat-still like photographs, but seen as moving from a moving car, and so psychologically there is "entertainment" value in this square box of unreality surrounded by the natural world, even though hot and monotonous, in the same way that matinee cinemas have "entertainment" value, because they cut up the daytime with night.

Many products are extolled on billboards. Some are offered for sale. Do the makers of these products really think that motorists will buy them, based on having seen the billboards? Obviously, the answer is no, for Coca-Cola is advertised in the middle of the jungle. What do they think, then? They must think they can wear us down, we who drive cars and who are defended by the fact of those cars, so that when we finally stop, out of gas or tired for the night or having reached our destination, we will be "broken" by the billboards and ready for surrender.

In much the same way, the King of the Edo and I sent many letters to each other during our last war, and these letters had the same purpose as those billboards on the highway: to send a message, broad and big and blunt, even insulting to the receiver; to influence the receiver so that he has subliminal sexing with the message, and to insure surrender at an unspecified later time and distance from the moment of billboard impact, even as he has temporarily surrendered his car, which was, in fact, his only shield against the message in the first place.

I found peculiar the idea of espousing philosophy through a billboard. One of the Christian churches offered the following BB, as I call them: MIRRORS SHOULD REFLECT A LITTLE BIT BEFORE THROWING BACK IMAGES. Especially odd was the following:

Paranoia:

The tree is well,

not sequoia.—Christian Science

I found nothing particularly Christian nor scientific about that BB. And then there are the BB's that have lapsed, peeled over time, exposed for what they are. These are blank BB's, and their message is: FOR SALE OR LEASE. CALL . . . And they give a telephone number, which is absurd, since, when one is driving, one barely has time to look at the billboard, never mind write down a telephone number. And yet there is something pathetic about these blank spaces in the middle of nature, and I have seen ordinary cars pulling off the road for the purpose of writing a number.

On Primitive Art:

When a foreign power comes to steal your house and wives and children, your land and water supply, your ordinary car or even your religion, you are aware of it. When he steals your art, you are *not* aware of it. And, if you are made aware of it, you forget it immediately, for oblivion is the caretaker of the mind and art is not something you eat, sleep or sex with. Still, I do have some opinions on the subject.

People who use the word "primitive" are naive, arrogant and mean-spirited in an exaggerated way, to hide the smallness of their cells. Trevor mentioned the name of Picasso. Think about this: in Nigeria we do not think of Best Western art as "civilized." So, why do Best Western artists project their own ignorance onto our masks, woodcuts, figurines and other artifacts? Is the idea of the artless, therefore, the pinnacle of art?

On the Charisma of Invisible Kings:

We were not sad to leave Lagos. We had had our fill of urban centers. A man can forget all too quickly how the grass savannas feel on bare feet in such crowded places. And I was prepared to die at the hands of the tall stranger Ajax, if death was what awaited me. But Ajax was sleeping when we returned, and I had not the heart to awaken him. When, after much feasting I brought my stool wives back to my bed, Ajax was gone. I looked at the length of ground he occupied and wondered why he had come, if not for assassination nor for shared wealth. I would have made him my heir-apparent. He was that tall. But I too was occupied with the ground he had covered, which I now filled with sexing and stool wives. And yet at one point between Stella and Della, I think, I seemed to awake from a deep sleep, and there in his full verticality Ajax towered over me. He was as steep as I was long and he looked like a mountain. And he whispered to me.

"He in whom I am well pleased, you are."

And then, what? Either he vanished or I fell back into the depths of stool-wife sleeping. And when I awoke the next morning, I could not swear to what had happened. But I think I was visited by the invisible regional king Achebe.

On Grief:

We had suffered these many casualties during our time of trial: three times three had died, three times eight had been wounded. And still, within the space of four full moons, thirty-three new pregnancies had been announced. I had in me too much the curse of clairvoyance to think these deaths and births were happenstance. Quite simply, the ground had been covered once more and fully.

Thinking, feeling, knowing this, I was still unprepared for death, which came so close it breathed when I breathed and echoed me in all my pain and ignorance.

First, my stool wife Keiko died. I must tell the truth here. She took her own life with a dagger in what is apparently the prescribed way. When all the other Japanese went home, she was left alone, forced by her marriage to me to stay. And, even though we shared many bodies together, the delights of which are still with me, her need for her father was stronger than her desire for me, and so she picked this spiritual way to return to her father and homeland.

Then my stool wife Naomi died. Her way was as slow as Keiko's was sudden. Naomi died of sleeping sickness. I could see her going, I could feel her going, but I was unable to go with her or bring her back. "Sleep peels," my fool Perry reminded me, and he spoke true, for there are many layers of the body to die before the whole is dead. Naomi shed her many layers one by one, until she was no longer with us but not yet apart from us.

Of the two deaths, I prefer the more sudden. The slow death requires a slow dying of everyone who watches. Each day I adjusted to the loss of her in a different way, a little more each day, until at last I was hollowed-out and holding her husk of shrunken skin and brittle bones. When the twig snaps, you remember this is not the tree. The same wood, the same wooden feeling in your hand, but not the tree, never again the whole tree.

And so my two stool wives, the last and most reluctant, the most passionate and mysterious, the ones who had never given me children, were no more. We recited their names in the litany of the lost, but I was uncalmed. What is a name next to a body?

I wandered drunk one night in my grieving out on the grass savannas, where only Trevor remained awake, insomniac that he was, chessing by moonlight. And he said to me, Kimbene, you know enough about loss now that you can play chess with me. And so I took up this game, one of the few games white men play that I admire, because it depends, not so much on strategies or expertise, but on an awareness of loss, a first-person feeling of hacked-off parts.

XVI

And just when you think there is nothing more to tell, there is something more to tell. This is in the nature of folk tales. They are as old as folk and equally long-winded.

The rural king Kimbene was eating a banana with his right hand, a lemon with his left, experiencing the bittersweetness of life, when the loyal Ngugi approached him.

"You have reached a crisis in your kingship," Ngugi said. "You have only two stool wives left. This is too plain. You must augment."

"I am still in mourning," Kimbene said. "I haven't the hardness for sexing new stools."

"Never mind. Kings are asked to make sacrifices for the good of their people."

"What would you have me do?"

"Choose two or three more. Enstool them."

"Will you help me choose?"

"Gladly."

"You never married, Ngugi?"

"It was not in my nature."

"Then you are the one green banana in the cluster of yellow and brown?"

"No, that is not in my nature either. I was born for scheming and dreaming. I am history's creature."

"You will get no grandchildren that way."

"Alas, no. Not even a persimmon."

After all this time together, Kimbene still could not fathom some of Ngugi's somersaults with language.

For the sake of solace, they drove the ordinary Volvo in circles, and when they were both feeling a bit of African vertigo they stopped and went to the basketball court, to watch Stella the stool wife instruct Kimbene's sons Mike and Moustafa in the finer points of the game. The boys at twelve had attained the height of six feet and three inches. But Stella still towered over them at six feet and eight inches. Her breasts and belly sagged from childbearing, but she could still do rim shots.

Kimbene and Ngugi stood behind a mahogany tree, so that they would not be seen. Stella was teaching the boys how to play the post.

"Get behind me," she said to Moustafa. "Lean into me, your knee against my back-of-knee. Yes, like that. Do you see how it forces me to bend? The zebras have eyes for your hands, especially if you fondle the buttocks of your adversary. And they have eyes for the ball. But they have no eyes for kneecaps. So now you think you have me? Watch what I do. I begin to dribble with my right hand, while I hook you with my left hand. Now the path is clear."

And she went around him for an easy lay-up. Then she turned to Moustafa.

"You just stand there?"

"You hooked me. I could do nothing."

"You could follow me. You could box me out for a rebound."

And she threw the ball into Moustafa's stomach. Hitting the boys with the ball was her way of emphasizing a point.

"Mike, you take the ball and I will defense you."

Mike began to lean into her. She held him up with her knee against the back of his leg. He began to dribble the ball with his right hand, but when he went to hook her with his left hand, she stepped back suddenly, he was still leaning, and he lost his balance and fell.

"Traveling," Stella shouted. "You have embarrassed yourself and the ball."

"But, Mama, you moved."

"Am I a statue, a fountainhead for pigeons? Am I not allowed to move? My ball. Now you defense me."

Mike stood behind her, feet spread apart, arms outstretched.

"I am going to shoot a sky hook," she said.

"Then I will block your shot," Mike said.

She turned on her left foot, the pivot foot, arched her right leg and let fly the hook. Mike never left

159

the ground to block it, for with her left hand she jabbed him in the stomach.

"I cry foul," he said, out of breath.

"Did you hear a whistle? Did you hear a whistle, Moustafa?"

"We don't have a whistle," Moustafa said.

"A technicality. What should he have done, Moustafa?"

"He should have stuck his fingers in your eyes. A blind shot has less chance of going in."

"Exactly. Now let's play a game. You two against me."

"You play too rough," Mike said. "I don't want to bleed today."

"Idiot. One day you will bloody me."

"Couldn't we just shoot free throws?" Moustafa asked.

"We're wasting time," Stella said. "I have cassava to stomp. Play ball."

"I'd like to see you play father one time," Mike said petulantly.

"Yes. What do you think would happen then?" Moustafa said.

"I would kick his butt," Stella said.

Kimbene did not appreciate this last remark. On the other hand, it was not proper for a rural king to shoot hoops with his stool wife, so there was no way of testing the veracity of her remark. He would have to let it pass. He was grateful to Stella for being such a tough taskmaster, since his sons were not old enough yet to warrant his attention.

"Do you think they will one day play in the

NBA?" Ngugi asked with some sarcasm in his voice.

"I care not a feather or a fig," Kimbene said. "They think it is the game they are being taught. But they are wrong. It is discipline they are learning. Stella has lost her looks, but her character soars. Their characters will have to soar even higher, and if they do, then one day they may be kings."

"They could be reading Shakespeare."

"When the Edo fight with Shakespeare, then we will all read Shakespeare."

Ngugi had no counter-argument, and so he kept quiet.

Then they went to spy on Della, the second stool wife, who was giving lessons in female etiquette to Kimbene's daughters Molly and Millie.

"So, if a young man speaks to you in Ibo dialect?"

"I answer him in Ibo dialectics," Molly said.

"And if he speaks to you in English?"

"I answer him in English," Millie said. "But I watch his verb conjugations very carefully."

"Excellent. And if a young man tells you that you have beautiful breasts?"

"I say, 'Thanks, yes, two of them,' " Molly said.

"Very good. And if you notice that one boy is much taller than the other boys?"

"I praise him for his tallness," Millie said.

"No, not necessarily. This will scare him away, for he will be awkward if he is tall and insecure about his height."

"Do boys break as easily as glass, then?" Millie asked.

"Yes. They are always a stone's throw away from being shattered."

"I'd like to cast the first stone," Millie said, giggling.

"Me too," Molly said.

"You haven't answered my question, girls."

"I would say he has excellent eyesight, strong hands, warrior's ways," Molly said. "I would tell him he is as wise and wide as he is tough and tall. I would use alliterations."

"That's it," Della said. "And if a fresh boy asks you to go out on the grass savannas with him?"

"Ask for a buffalo escort?"

"Insist upon a group excursion?"

"Tell him he's mislaid his fetish stick in his loincloth?"

"Ask him if he irrigates the land with his face?"

"Offer passive resistance?"

"Go for the golden stool?"

"No, you nanas, you must thank him for such a flattering offer. Tell him you will ask your mother and father and give him an answer in a day or two. He will go away quietly."

"Can we really start having children when we are twelve?" Millie asked.

"Yes, you are biologically equipped then."

"Will it hurt very much?"

"Yes, very much. But there are oils to soothe the pain and keep the cavities from squeaking."

"And do we ever get to play with dolls?"

"No, these are only used in cultures in which child-bearing is deferred."

"What else must we know?"

"When the time comes, I will teach you how to grunt. You must know how to grunt. For today I will teach you how to serve tea."

"Is this really necessary?" Millie asked. "I have never seen you serve tea."

"It's something I had to learn as a little girl, because the British were still here. It became part of the canon then. It has never been questioned sufficiently to be taken out."

"But nobody likes tea," Molly said.

"Trevor likes tea. You can practice on him."

"At least, it's better than what we learned last week," Millie said.

"Ugh. Stains!" said Molly.

"Cleaning a man's undergarments is something women have done since temporality," Della said.

"They should have to clean ours," Millie giggled.

Molly agreed with giggling.

"Maybe one day they will," Della said. "That's why the world is round and not flat."

"I thought it was for balancing baskets on your head," Millie said.

"You must marry into different tribes," Della said. "The two of you together would be too much for any husband."

"I'm going to marry Uncle Ngugi when I grow up," Molly said.

"Your father will pick for you when the time comes," Della said.

Kimbene and Ngugi were satisfied. They had heard enough.

"Your stool wives are fine teachers," Ngugi said. "Your children are fine pupils."

"Everything seems to be going smoothly," Kimbene said.

"And yet you do not seem happy?"

"I thought after grief there would be new life, new passion, more purpose. Instead, there are stones in my heart. I am merely bored."

"You must choose new stool wives."

"And then?"

"And then we must find a way to rekindle your ambitions."

"But I have everything a rural king can have."

"There are other types of kings besides rural kings."

"You must not speak such seditions. And yet I have to tell you that suddenly I am not bored."

"Taboos were invented for this very purpose."

When Kimbene informed his people that he would be taking on new stool wives, Stella and Della bit their lips, but the rest of the tribe cheered vociferously, all in a rhythm, hooting, paraphrasing owls.

The one exception was Perry Lumumba, who lost all composure and began reciting a string of palindromes that made no sense, not even for a rational rural king.

"Al lets Della call Ed Stella."

"Sun is sinus."

"Viva let Tel Aviv."

164

"Slag gals."

"Lie veil."

He would have gone on, but Kimbene ordered that he be bound and gagged, sedated with kola nuts and beet broth, leeched and brought back to his senses.

"There will be no more talk of scoria and nasal passages," Kimbene said, glad that the outbursts of his fool had firmed him in his resolve.

Out of respect for his stool wives Stella and Della, Kimbene went outside of his tribe and looked for new stool wives among the neighboring Ibo nations. He came back with three, named Mary, Diana and Florence, who were enstooled with great pomp and circumstance, to the musical accompaniment of Otis Redding and Paganini.

XVII

Offspring are not enough. Health, wealth and offspring are not enough. Sometimes a rural king needs more than a *bon ton* manicure, a chest of drawers full of coral beads and unlimited sexing with five different stool wives to feel fulfilled. He needs a good war, a useless hobby that consumes him or a sense of history. Vox clamoris, it came to Kimbene that he should build a library, which he did, and dedicate the libary as he would a stool wife, which he did, and donate the first tome, which he did, in the form of a first edition of *Things Fall Apart.*

And then the news came, not by courier, newspaper or radio, but by drums, that Morse code of tam-tams from tribe to tribe, that the regional king had either died or disappeared, which in this case amounted to a tautology, and that all the rural kings were being summoned, were being called to convene for the purpose of choosing a new regional king.

"Your moment is at hand," Ngugi said.

"You jest, Ngugimahn. This is not wily Joe Odoki. It will take more than elevator shoes against a baobab tree this time. All these kings are tall."

"Just so. Physical appearances will mean nothing. But psychological appearances may add an inch or two."

"I don't understand."

"It is better that you do not, for you might show the ruse on your face. Prepare yourself, your best ornamental dressing and many gifts to give your brethren. Leave the stool wives to me."

"This is a strange request."

"Have I ever failed you?"

"Never. But can you say without prevarication that we will prevail?"

"If government can design a thing so small."

Kimbene had no idea what that meant, and so he went to the convening with height and innocence, his best weapons. At the table of great feasting sat seventeen rural kings and their stool wives, all festooned, garlanded and laid out. Behind them scurried short men of note, like Ngugi, spreading rumors and taking bets about who would be the next crowned king. They hissed and buzzed like insects. They pranced and cavorted, they rumored and wagered, they mocked the anteater's tongue with silky epithets and sticky riddles and other self-promotions. Ngugi came away with acclaim for his walking recitations of Shakespeare. Black men with

168

British names and tight *perruques* offered him snuff or ragtime, but he refused. To one named Butts he proclaimed that his favorite Shakespearean character was Coriolanus. To another named Dobbins he said, "My kingdom for a horse." And to a third named Moore, he said, "Othello, dear fellow?" He was in his element.

When it came time to toast the invisibly absent Achebe, all the seventeen rural kings stood, looked at each other and hoisted their gourds on high, while the stool wives sat and said nothing. And then they took a secret ballot. Kimbene was pronounced to be the new regional king, with two votes. Fifteen other kings had received one vote each.

After great feasting, full of toasting and boasting and sworn allegiances to Kimbene, they all returned to their respective tribes in ordinary cars, all except Kimbene, who sat stunned and amazed, unable to find chalk enough in his knee-caps to stand. The parquet varnish on the picnic table glistened in the sun like a scored sinus, reflecting the face of the new regional king with a butterscotch melt. His face lay there before him in a patchwork pool like a veiled lie.

The stool wives, now lax with lassitude after so much posing, sat in various stages of deshabille and gradual undressing around him, swatting flies and humming hymns of indifference. Their boredom was in stark contrast with the cockalorum of wild birds, the cornucopia of many fruits, the teeming canvas of many colors in that idyllic place.

169

Only Ngugi seemed to know what to do next. What he did next was to sit down to stupor with his king.

"How is it possible, Ngugimahn?" Kimbene asked. "I am stunned and amazed."

"It was simple, my lord."

"Was I that much taller than anyone else?"

"You seemed so, my lord."

"But how?"

"I sawed off the stools of your stool wives, my lord. By one-sixth, each stool. The consequence was that they sat lower and of course you stood taller. I knew that most of these rural kings would vote for themselves. As it turned out I needed to convince just one of them that you were indeed taller."

"But which one?"

"Does it matter? He knows who he is. He will spend a lifetime thinking about this day."

"And my stool wives. Did they not know something was different?"

"I drugged them, each and all. That is why you see them thus, with porous personalities."

"You are truly magnificent, Ngugimahn. I thank you, from a heart that is bottomless. But now I am feeling sunstruck. Let us go home, brother."

"You are home."

"What do you mean?"

"You are the new regional king. This is home. You cannot return to your rural tribe."

"But they will be without a king."

"They must find another."

"Surely we can drive back for my belongings and for goodbye feasting with my people?"

"Neither. Do you see those two strong men over there? They are your chauffeurs. But I must tell you, the regional king does not drive an ordinary car."

"So I will get a Mercedes, I suppose?"

"No. You will sit atop a palanquin, which those two will carry. Their names are Al and Ed."

"No more car?"

"No car, no feasting among the people, for that would put you too close to them and make you mortal in their eyes. No more speaking in dialect. Henceforth, you will have a personal linguist, just as Sosa was for Achebe. This man behind me is named Okolo, whose name means "the voice." He will be your personal linguist. He will translate everything you say, for your words are not to be heard directly. Unfortunately, his chosen language is French, which would be fine in Senegal, but on this side of Africa is not in much demand. This is why he was available."

Kimbene looked at him and noted that the man seemed to be talking to himself. Each time Kimbene spoke, the man spoke, with a slight time lag between them, like an echo.

"You know, Ngugi, I wasn't expecting this."

"Tu sais, Ngugi, je n'y attendais pas," Okolo said.

"Don't listen to him," Ngugi said, "if you don't want to hear, but he is required to translate just the same. He is useless for conversation and will not dialogue with you. He has no words of his own. Your words give him license to speak, and this is his only license to speak."

"How strange," Kimbene said.

"Comme c'est drôle," Okolo said.

"And my stool wives?" Kimbene asked.

Ngugi had to speak louder to make himself heard above the translation of Okolo.

"I will have new stools made for them."

"That's not what I meant. Am I to live alone like this?"

"You may have anyone you wish live with you."

"Will you stay with me?"

"Of course. That is why I never married."

"And my fool Perrymahn?"

"He is still quite crazy and has lost his speech. But if he heals, he can come."

"And Trevor?"

"It is irregular to have a white man living in the entourage of a regional king, but your powers are beyond questioning, so I think it can be arranged."

"Have you told me everything?"

"Almost everything."

"You have saved the worst for last?"

"Or the best. I don't know which."

"Speak plainly."

"The regional king cannot refuse new stool wives. Since he embodies all that is fertile, he must receive all vessels of fertility: namely, new stool wives. He must accept up to nine wives."

"I can barely feed the five I have now."

"Material wealth will not be a problem. All the rural kings will pay tributes. Food and clothing are, thus, taken care of. But you are on your own for sexing. And you are expected to increase and multiply."

"I may be on my back for the rest of my life."

"It is the dream of every king to be thus."

"Then why do I feel such tremendous loss?"

"You are breathing new air, which few will ever breathe. You are no longer part of your people, but rather above them, just as the eagle flies above the crow."

"But I was happy as a rural king . . ."

"Mais j'étais content d'être un roi de campagne . . ."

"I could drink and dance, I could toast and boast, I could touch my people and be touched. I could tell jokes, make puns, get ready for neighborhood wars. And now you tell me I cannot do these things."

"No, you are too powerful. You are quite invisible now."

"Who would have believed it?"

"Qui l'eût cru?"

"Shut up, Okolo."

"Tais toi, Okolo."

"I may go mad, Ngugi."

"No one will know if you do."

"Well, let's walk to this fine house and have a fine bath. Can we do this?"

"I will walk. You must be carried by Al and Ed."

And so it was done. Kimbene sat on the palan-

173

quin and was hoisted up by Al and Ed, who carried him in this manner to the house of the regional king. When he was let down, Kimbene bent over and threw up all his food and drink.

"What is the matter?" Ngugi said.

"I'm afraid of heights," the regional king said.

"J'ai du vertige," Okolo said.

And when Kimbene stooped to gag some more, Okolo bent over and gagged with him, even though it was clear to everyone that Okolo wasn't feeling the least bit nauseous. So diligent was he at his task that he either lacked all empathy or possessed too much of it.

Kimbene was both embarrassed and frustrated, and he wished to focus both on Okolo, who dogged him like moss dogs trees. So he whispered into Ngugi's ear. Okolo whispered as well, even though he had no words to say.

"Chuchotements . . ."

"This is a bit unkingly of you," Ngugi said to Kimbene. "He is no more than your aural reflection. If he loses face, you lose face. He is not the other. There is no battle to be fought with him."

Kimbene disagreed, but didn't say as much. He chose to keep silent, especially since another round of food was coming up his throat.

In the months that followed, Kimbene was a veritable shut-in. He had no stomach for repeated trips on the palanquin. Consequently, he had time for sexing and stool wives, even though they seemed estranged from him. Stella and Della were not happy to leave the tribe. Mike, Moustafa, Millie

174

and Molly were all homesick for their friends and complained bitterly that they had no one to play with. Al and Ed got down on their knees and pretended to be children, but the real children were not amused. Mary, Diana and Florence seemed more like extra furniture than like people with feelings. They maintained their eyes of twilight sleep and watched television for hours on end.

And then the extra stool wives came: Hannah from Johannesburg, with stories of censure and abridgment; Cindi, a white woman from Poughkeepsie, who had come to Africa as a hippie in the Sixties and had never gone back; Miriam, a prostitute from Lagos, who said she was drawn to this place from a reading of the Tarot cards; and Esther from Tel Aviv, who called the rest of the stool wives "slag gals." All of them adjusted reasonably well to the lazy laissez-faire life of stool wife, save for Esther, who insisted upon kosher cassava, which was a foreign concept for all the other stool wives, for whom cassava was either poisonous or it was not.

One morning when Okolo overslept, Kimbene hurried to Ngugi for a private conversation.

"We should not be meeting like this," Ngugi said.

"Don't be a stinkermahn for rules. I have craved this personal talk. What does power feel like to you, Ngugi?"

"It feels like a full stomach, a clear head, bowels that flow like rivers. What does it feel like to you?"

"It feels lonely. Like a cloud."

175

"Even with all your stool wives?"

"Especially with them. I feel like a freak of men among women. I am surrounded by women who talk to each other and the echo of Okolo, who mirrors me with words I cannot understand. I have no foes, and so of what value are my friends? I feel simply byzantine."

"What more could you want?"

"What is above regional king, since I seem fated to climb this ladder?"

"It breaks down after this. There are no more kingships. There is parliament in Lagos, military positions, presidencies. But these are not kingships. Like in England."

"And what do they do, after they have done it all?"

"They retire to estates like this one and write their memoirs. They travel from time to time. They wait to be asked questions. Then they die, I suppose."

"I have learned a word of Okolo's language. It is called cul-de-sac. Cul is the word for anus. The rest means "blocked up." I have reached the cul-de-sac of kingship."

"There are cruelties, corruptions, perversions and decadences you have not tried. Some kings wander into these domains."

"Then do you recommend I wander into these domains?"

"No. I recommend you live long and prosper, leaving many grandchildren behind you."

"Do you think that women come to the same crisis as kings?"

"How should they?"

"Having had children and seeing their whole lives before them like a lake . . . that kind of crisis?"

"I don't know. I've never asked them."

"Maybe we live too long these days. Our ancestors died in wars. They had no time for idle minds. You see, Ngugi, the more stool wives I have, the less appetite I keep. I have put into all of them, except for Esther, who teases me and tells me stories instead. But I have stopped thinking of sexing. Maybe I could go back to being rural king."

"You can never go back that way."

"Then history is not palindromic."

"No, not in these matters."

"I wish I had my fool here to distract me. I would like to hear one good palindrome before I cross the great river."

"Put your mind to better things, Kimbene."

"You know, Ngugimahn, I began to write down the history of my kingship last week, but I couldn't find words. All I could find were names, and these names were the litany of the lost: wily Joe Odoki, Libidoki, Caruso, Fairfax, Kampala, Keiko, Naomi."

Ngugi read to his king and stroked his hair until Okolo came to translate. Kimbene would not give him this satisfaction. He went back to bed instead.

XVIII

A cockatoo awoke Ngugi at dawn's early light. He couldn't decide if the sound came from a free bird or from one of the many caged birds in the otherwise quiet kingdom of the regional monarch Kimbene. Ngugi arose from his bed and, plain to see, he had grown quite fat for an Ibo. Food and sleep, uninterrupted by sexing or war, can do this to a man, even in the tropics. Temporality has the same effects, but the process is more invisible.

He heard noises on the verandah and went to see, as though seeing noises were a natural thing. There he found Kimbene, a banana in his right hand, a lemon in his left, grimacing, first in a Munch-Modigliani North-South fashion from bites on the banana, then in a Klimt-Kandinsky East-West fashion from sucks on the lemon.

"What are you doing, my lord?"

"I am trying to think of a surd."

179

"What is a surd?"

"A voiceless sound."

"That's absurd."

"Exactly."

He was still trying to confound the echo Okolo, whose name means "the voice" and nothing else.

Ngugi wondered at the equation, inverse in this case, between the amount of power achieved and the preoccupations that followed. Did Napolean at Elba wonder about the exact definition of pi? Did Hannibal, crossing the Pyrenees, think about the circumference of elephant ears? Did Martin Luther King Junior think about papal infallibility when he had his dream?

After a full day of naps and foreign dignitaries, Kimbene found Trevor on the verandah chessing.

"Where is Okolo?" Trevor asked.

"I gave orders to Al and Ed to tie him to a chair."

"A regal decision, I'm sure."

"Do you think any of those foreign devils I saw had a soul?"

"Unlikely," Trevor said. "I think they're required to turn them in when they enter the foreign service. I know I was."

"And do you miss it?"

"Good question. How shall I answer? More than a missing finger, but less than a migraine."

"I like chess-playing."

"You've gotten bloody good at it. You give me bashing after bashing."

"Perhaps you let me win?"

"Not on your life. I may observe the other amenities, but I draw the line at chess. You simply have a natural gift for it."

"I like it that kings have queens instead of stool wives. And I like moving backwards and forwards. Chess is so palindromic."

"So why are you complaining?"

"I miss losing. It has been many many moons and I have forgotten how it feels."

"Ha. You make me think of Duchamp."

"Do chomp?"

"No. Duchamp, as in shampoo."

"You Americans speak in funny ways."

"Kim, I've been wanting to tell you this for years . . ."

"If it has to do with being British, I have no ears to hear it."

"Thank you. Then I have no tongue to speak it. But I do have a gift for you. Got it from one of the dignitaries."

"What is this thing?"

"It's a potato."

"Ah yes, the edible tuber."

"I suggest you eat it au gratin, but suit yourself."

"I will have one of the stool wives cook it."

Kimbene took the potato into the kitchen, where he found Della giving etiquette lessons to his daughters.

"Della. This is potato. It is an edible tuber, just like cassava. Cook it for me."

Then he went back to chessing and talking with Trevor.

181

"I miss playing out on the grass savannas in the darkness," Kimbene said.

"You are the sentimental one, aren't you? I thought I missed it too, but then I remembered all the bugs and mosquitoes, and I remembered the howling of nearby animals scaring the hell out of me, and I remembered all the times I got so potted that I fell on the board and scattered the men and ruined several perfectly good games that way. But are you saying you'd like to go back out there sometime?"

"Yes."

"Maybe with a bottle of brandy?"

"Yes."

"Well, then, old boy, I accept your challenge. I used to win out there."

"Tonight after sexing," Kimbene said.

When he went back to the kitchen, the potato was ready. Della and his daughters had stomped on it, beaten it with mortar and pestle, pounded it with wooden gourds and then boiled it. The boiling blistered the crystals into a singed crispness and scalded baldness, the likes of which he had never seen.

"How is?" Della asked.

"Like sand," Kimbene said. "I prefer cassava."

"Rebut tuber," Della said.

"Thank you, Della. I needed that."

"Shall I throw this grist to the wind, along with caution?"

"No. Put it in the next soup."

"But it will drown. It will sink to the bottom and stick to the pot."

"It needs a fastener."

Della sent the daughters to look for a rasp, a hasp, a clasp, any fastener.

"Will you be needing me for sexing this night?"

"I think not. I'll try again with Esther."

"It's been five years."

"I'm in no hurry."

"She says she is a princess."

"Do you believe her?"

"She says all women in Tel Aviv are princesses, even the brown ones like her. I do not believe this."

"Good. You have sense, Della. Tell me, are you ever jealous?"

"No."

"And would you tell me if you were?"

"No."

"Good. Say no to drugs."

"I will."

"Say hi to Stella."

"I will."

"We will have gray hair together."

"Yes. May I tell you a secret?"

"I wish you would."

"I have been sexing Trevor. On nights when you don't need me. Are you jealous?"

"No. I am grateful. I wish someone would sex Okolo."

"It will never happen. He is all talk and no action."

183

"Good novels are thus. Bad novels are the reverse."

"I don't read novels."

Kimbene went to bed with Esther, who teased him and told him stories of blood and first-born massacres, of plagues of frogs and boils and things that go boomp in the night.

She was very good with words, and Kimbene let her go on with her stories, even though he had heard them all before.

"I have been told you are a princess," he said at last, when there was a lull in the story-telling.

"I am a princess, yes."

"And does a princess ever spread her legs for a man?"

"Almost never."

"Why is this?"

"She is always too tired or afflicted or cramped or bored or jealous or angry or not rich enough or in some other way involved with mirrors and narcissism."

"And what is she afraid of, that she will never spread her legs?"

"Of losing the only thing she has of any value."

"But if she could take it back afterwards and it increased in value, two-fold or twenty-fold, what then?"

"This would be a different slant altogether."

"And if she looked to her heritage, all the stories that make her, and saw that the Red Sea, itself, spread its legs and parted, so that all the people of the world could pass over, would that not consti-

tute a form of cultural precedent for future reen-
àctments?"

"It would indeed."

"And if she were ever asked, she could always
say that she held out longer than any other stool
wife ever held out, so much longer in fact that no
one would ever believe she surrendered, and her
holding out could be kept psychologically into per-
petuity?"

"Yes, the point would have been made, regardless of the outcome."

"And could she not, if she still felt certain qualms
of conscience, spread her legs only half as wide as
other women, so that she might maintain her status
as princess?"

"Or even half of half."

"Yes, the spreading could be quite unconscious."

"Oh, it would be, I assure you."

"Just so, even as now. A metaphor is good for
repression. Let's say you are a horseshoe and I am
a stake."

"Like this?"

"Yes, like this."

"What now?"

"Ring me."

And she did.

Much later, Kimbene stole himself away from his
bed, to go play chess with Trevor out on the grass
savannas. Unfortunately, Okolo, Al and Ed were
still awake, so they had to play on top of the palanquin, with Al and Ed holding them up and mut-
tering things about chess not being as fast as check-

185

ers or backgammon. Three men and a chess board on top of a palanquin in total darkness with many mosquitoes does not make for an enviable evening, but both Kimbene and Trevor had just been sexed and they numbed their senses with brandy and even Okolo got potted to the point that he fell off the palanquin and passed out and Kimbene looked over and remembered that he was afraid of heights and threw up on his interpreter and Al and Ed laughed so hard that they passed gas which heat of course was wont to rise and their laughter shook the palanquin so much that all the chess pieces changed positions as did the strategies and possible outcomes and they stayed this way until morning and Al and Ed had sunk to their knees with exhaustion and Kimbene and Trevor had both passed out on top of each other, checkmating themselves instead of their pieces. Okolo woke up dizzy and confounded, remembering only that the word for chess in French is the same as the word for failure. Al and Ed suffered from shin splints and had to be carried to bed. Kimbene and Trevor woke up with the rain king in their brains, bloodshot as beggar's sandals, puffy and bulbous from brandy and mosquito bites. And the mosquitoes inflated to three times their normal engorgement, full of the hemal history of the Ibo, so much so that they couldn't fly, and if they did they exploded.

"I could not enjoy myself more," Kimbene said.

"Je ne pourrais pas m'amuser davantage," Okolo said, stumbling to the task of translation.

"Me neither," Trevor said.

186

"Moi non plus," Okolo said.

And then Ngugi came to interrupt their frivolity, and he insisted upon a private audience with Kimbene, which was unlike him, since he usually stood up for Okolo. Kimbene gladly granted this request, and Okolo did not object, for he was used to bondage by now.

Kimbene and Ngugi went inside one of the closets inside the house and closed the door behind them.

"What is it, Ngugimahn?"

"The news is grave, very grave. There is a war between our former tribe and the neighboring Edo, and this time it is a bloody war. Many have died on both sides."

"Why do they fight?"

"Farmers heard groaning and gurgling beneath the ground. There was talk of new oil. Both tribes dispute the ownership of the land. So now they are killing each other. Leopold the leper has been killed twice."

"How is that possible?"

"He was killed once vertically. Then when he went horizontal he was killed again."

"Then his name shall appear twice in the litany of the lost," Kimbene decreed. "Twice-told Leopold."

"There are more. Brother Jero has been beheaded. And many more besides."

"Who is king of our tribe now?"

"You know full well, for he pays his tributes in triplicate. Lon Nol Lumumba."

187

"A bloodthirsty boy. I never realized how tall he was."

"He has his brothers stretch him daily. He is over seven feet tall and can slam-dunk with either hand."

"Peace will not come cheaply with him as rural king. I could destool him . . ."

"It would look bad in the middle of a war."

"And who is king of the Edo now?"

"The blind boy Tyree."

"That little whisper of a man?"

"He has grown to a mountain."

"What happened to confusion and admiration? King Friday and I were able to wage wars without casualties."

"They have gone the way of the baobab tree," Ngugi said. "Technology has rendered them impotent. The people have guns now."

"Both sides?"

"Both. They say the superpowers sell directly."

"And if I do nothing?"

"They will decimate each other. Already they use women and children for shields."

"Shameful."

"And there is always the risk that the war could spread to other tribes."

"Which would endanger my tributes."

"That is one consequence, yes."

"Then I must talk to Lon Nol. He will listen."

"You are forbidden to talk directly to him. You are invisible to him now. He would only listen to Okolo."

"That blunt instrument?"

"I'm afraid so."

"What are the chances of success in that?"

"Slim, if I may use the name of a disease."

"But I am not forbidden to speak directly to the king of the Edo?"

"It would be irregular and only effective as a last resort."

"Then I must send you, Ngugi, and Okolo to speak to both sides. Wear a white flag."

"What shall I say, by way of Okolo?"

"Say that I insist that all killing cease. If the black blood indeed boils over again, both sides shall profit as equal partners."

"Shall I go now, then?"

"Untie Okolo first."

This he did and they went with Kimbene's blessings. Try as he might, Kimbene could not duplicate either the sexing or the chessing of the previous night. He was too preoccupied with the peace. Visions of Achebe haunted his dreams: a death never verified, a disappearance neither proven nor disbelieved, no clue, no motive, no fair or foul play, and only temporality to make it so. Kimbene awakened each morning, wondering why a regional king would vanish at the height of his power, where he would go to, and how might those left behind handle such an enigma. Kimbene awakened each morning with the growing belief that his predecessor still lived somewhere, and, truth be told, he wondered not about the reasons why, for he, himself, was filled with reasons why, but curiously and ever more steadily how he might follow in his kingfather's footsteps.

One week later Okolo returned without Ngugi. Okolo came back stumbling, with bloody welts across his face and arms, making clicking sounds with his throat, the kind hanged men or night cicadas make. And then, minimus glottis, Kimbene saw what had been done. Someone had severed the tongue of his translator. Kimbene tried to ascertain which side had done this deed, but Okolo didn't know, for he could not tell an Ibo blade from an Edo blade. Nor could he say what had happened to Ngugi. After many mimes, presuppositions and charades-gaming, Kimbene pieced together the following story: they had been separated in the very fields under dispute; Okolo had been captured, beaten and further separated from his tongue, perhaps under the provocation of his own French-speaking; and, while his captors went off in pursuit of Ngugi, he had freed himself and escaped, hoping that Ngugi would also escape and find his way back.

Kimbene ordered Okolo to bed, and he waited three days for the return of Ngugi. When he did not return Kimbene resolved to find out why.

"Trevor, I fear they have killed my best boy. Will you risk life and limb and come with me?"

"Yes, of course. But are you sure this is wise? You could stay at home and order whole armies in to tame this fire. You could even say it's a civil war, I dare say, and ask the militia in Lagos to intervene."

"I could do all of these things."

"And, worse, aren't you breaking some rules?"

"All of them. I go without bodyguards or palanquin. I go without interpretation. I meddle in what does not concern me. And I risk being visible to mere mortals who might kill me and their entire belief system with me."

"Why then?"

"Because it is the way of the world and because I made the mistake of sending Ngugi in my place, and he was my best beloved. And I need you to tell me, if you can, if there is more oil there."

"I'm an oil man, not a magician. I may not be able to tell you anything without proper equipment and adequate samples."

"You will put your ear to the earth and know, one way or the other. I give you this power and it shall be."

"Okay, then. Let me get a spot of tea to steady my nerves and we'll be off."

Kimbene readied himself for war. He stripped down to loincloth and took his machete and spear. Trevor packed his chess set and a bottle of brandy. And they set out.

Trevor was in fact astonished. Like some zoo tiger let loose in the wilds, Kimbene sloughed off his years of kingship and became an agile warrior again. He took paths with purpose, found food when they were hungry and seemed to get stronger the closer they got to their destination.

"I named this place," he said when they had

reached the outskirts of his former tribe, now fortified with a stake fence, animal traps and gun turrets. "It still belongs to me."

But his former tribe did not recognize its once tall rural king. The sentries sighted his tall silhouette and began firing their rifles at him. Kimbene disbelieved bullets and would have walked on, but Trevor had the presence of mind to pull him back and out of range.

"They cannot kill me, you know," Kimbene said to Trevor. "I am certain of this now."

"Forgive me, Kim, but I was less certain."

"It used to be that I could walk this ground as an ordinary man, and they could smell my sweat and hear my humor and see my height and know I was their master. Now they have lost their smells and measure distance with these bullets."

"Crazy as this sounds, we might do better with the other side. Hear my logic. If it is taboo for you to walk as an ordinary man among your people, then your doing so will accomplish nothing. They will try to shoot you as a stranger, they will never recognize you for who you really are, you will have made them all crazy for nothing, and the war will go on."

"All this is as you say."

"Then let us cross the fields and go to the Edo, who may well be so confounded and amazed at your boldness that they will strike no blows and offer no resistance."

"You speak like Ngugimahn."

"Maybe his spirit moves through me."

192

They began to make their way across the fields, side-stepping many bodies along the way.

"These dead will be mulch for the next harvest," Kimbene said.

At dawn's early light they came upon a clearing in which stood a cross, a crucifix upon which was affixed the rotting body of Ngugi, minus the head, which lay at the base of the cross. Trevor looked up at the corpse on the cross. Kimbene looked down at the head.

"I am clairvoyant, after all," Kimbene said with tears in his eyes. "They have killed my best boy."

"The bastards. But which side did this?"

"It does not matter, or I would know this too. What matters is the deed, not the intention or the actual assassin. In the mind of the regional king, both sides are culpable and both will pay in blood."

"There's a piece of paper with writing on it. Seems like Latin to me."

"Read it."

" 'SUBI DURA A RUDIBUS.' "

"Spell it."

This Trevor did, even though spelling seemed a retrogression upon reading.

"I have no truck with dead languages," Kimbene said. "Do you know its meaning?"

"It's been a long time since I had Latin at Leeds."

"I grant you full recall."

"Then yes, I can translate. It means: 'ENDURE ROUGH TREATMENT FROM BARBARIANS.' "

"Then we have both meanings."

"I beg your pardon?"

"The language may be dead, but the letters are not. This is also a palindrome. The palindrome tells me my former fool and all his family have betrayed me. The translation tells me the Edo are equally to blame, for we always called them barbarians when we were children."

"We must avenge Ngugi," Trevor said.

"We must bury him. This alone separates us from the beasts in the forest, to which we always aspire to become: we alone stop what we are doing and bury our dead."

"But these fields are reeking with unburied dead."

"These savages have forgotten. But we have not forgotten. I will open the earth with my machete and make a bed for my Ngugi. While I do this, you must put your ear to the ground and tell me true about the oil."

When Kimbene had finished burying his childhood friend, Trevor was decided.

"There's no oil. Maybe natural gas or something else, but no oil."

"I could have predicted as much."

"You must feel very powerful."

"Clairvoyance is like mystical gymnastics. You do the splits, with one leg in this world, the other in another. Ngugi was my last attachment here. My predecessor haunts me there."

"Sounds rash. Don't go batty on me, old boy."

"Exactly the opposite. You are one of my best weapons."

They moved into the Edo camp in full view of the

Edo warriors, who were stupefied by their audacity. And, because they did not act defensively, they met no resistance. There were minor attempts, mostly indignities, nothing atrocious. Some Edo warriors tried to spit on them, but sudden winds produced boomeranging wetness on their own faces. Other Edo tried to butt them with spears, but their elbows recoiled as in epileptic fits and they butted themselves. Gunsights fogged mysteriously, triggers jammed, machetes became as unwieldy as medicine balls. But no atrocities.

Kimbene walked straight up to Tyree.

"You have grown exceedingly tall, blind boy."

"Could this be the voice of Kimbene, the once powerful king of the Ibo?"

"My compliments."

"I never forget a voice. You break all rules of decency coming here."

"I sent my best boy and personal linguist, but they were both mistreated."

"I cannot comment on that. I saw nothing."

His whole tribe laughed with him. Kimbene wondered how he had once felt sorry for this brat-bully.

"Your eyes have not grown with you, I see."

"On the contrary. I can pierce a man's heart at forty paces. Would you honor me with a personal demonstration?"

"Of course. I am always in the mood for miracles."

"I don't think this is such a hot idea," Trevor said, whispering to Kimbene.

"I must let him play his game before I play mine. It would be impolite to refuse. We will teach this sassy boy some manners."

Kimbene stood back to back with Tyree, then walked off forty paces and turned. Tyree waited and finally turned as well, the dagger in his hand.

"My heart now," Kimbene warned. "Not my head or feet."

"I can hear you ticking from here," Tyree said, hurling the knife.

It would indeed have pierced the heart of the regional king, if Kimbene had not put up his right hand to stop it. The knife went through the palm of his hand and stuck. He pulled it out, and where the knife was there was now a stigmatum, but no gaudy show of blood.

"May I return your blade?"

"Of course," Tyree said, somewhat surprised that Kimbene still had voice. He knew his aim was true, he heard his knife break skin, and he could not understand how Kimbene could still address him.

"Have you broken all your rules to come begging for your people?"

"Regional kings do not beg," Kimbene said. "You must know that. I have come to tell you there is no oil. You must stop fighting."

"You are the master of deceit," Tyree said. "Why should I believe you?"

"Because I have brought my oilman Trevor with me. He has listened to the earth and there is no oil.

You will not listen to me, but I must tell you anyway."

"Your oilman was ill advised to come with you. He will die a horrible death. I personally will eat his brains."

"Do you play chess, Tyree?"

"Of course. I have no equal among the Edo kings."

"Then I challenge you to play my oilman at chess. If you win you may kill us both with my blessings. If you lose, then you must grant me a private audience."

"Agreed. I will be honored either way. When the regional king of the Ibo asks for a personal audience with but a rural king of the Edo, this is an admission of the weakness of the Ibo."

"Why don't you play him, yourself?" Trevor asked. "You've gotten much better at chess than I am."

"It would be beneath me to sit at table with this inferior boy. You will find that he plays aggressively and attacks straight-ahead, but he defends peripherally. You will use this information to beat him."

It took three days, with many interruptions, long pauses and move counts, but Trevor finally bested Tyree, as Kimbene knew he would, for a man who knows loss will always prevail against an aggressive assassin. This is why detective novels are written.

Tyree was confused and humiliated in front of his

whole tribe, who didn't understand a thing about chess, but did understand a thing or two about nervous twitchy kings.

"You have brought this white neo-colonial to insult me. I shall let my personal crows have your eyeballs for breakfast, Kimbene."

"You are not as hospitable with me as I once was with you. Do you still have the sunglasses I gifted you?"

"No. They made me look like Ray Charles. I smashed them to pieces."

"What about my personal audience?"

"In my tent."

They both went inside Tyree's war tent.

"You know, Tyree, the old saw is true. Pride cometh before a fall."

"What lions say?"

"You have wit and height and viciousness."

"And soon I will have Ibo slaves, oil wells and your head on top of my umbrella."

"Then I must strike a bargain with you for my safety and that of my oilman. And if you would gamble with me, I must strike a bargain for an end to this witless war in which real people die real deaths."

"More tricks, Kimbene?"

"Only if you let me. A clever man cannot be tricked."

"Then what is your bargain?"

Kimbene knew that he could always wound Tyree in his pride. He was invulnerable in every other way.

"First, I will give you what you can never have. It will shame you. Then I will give you what you can never have, and it will exalt you, so much so that Trevor and I will leave this place without a hand upon us."

"Ha," Tyree boasted, "I refuse to believe the first and I have given orders to prevent the second."

"I have withstood your weapon. I have bested you at chess with my man Trevor. If now I can accomplish what I have said, will you then be persuaded?"

"Of course," Tyree lied.

"Then let me put you at your ease with an extra delight. May I approach your ear?"

"I must feel your hands and belt and mouth first."

Tyree was feeling for weapons. Kimbene made fists of his hands and let Tyree touch him everywhere.

"You may approach," he said at last.

"Then tell me what you hear," Kimbene said, and he bit his lower lip with his upper teeth and exhaled sharply through the hole in his hand.

"It is the sound of a baby crying," Tyree said.

"No, it is only me, warming my hand with wet spittle and breathing."

Tyree immediately licked his own hand and blew on it, but it produced no such sound.

"This is a carnival trick. I am not shamed."

"Then listen again and tell me what you hear."

Kimbene moved away from him and Tyree stood,

listening intently. What he heard were sharp clicking noises.

"It sounds like a man whose tongue has been cut."

"No," Kimbene said, getting up. "It was the sound of my ebony bone, hammering the wet fur-hole of your eldest daughter."

"Impossible," Tyree said. "How is it possible?"

"I cast a spell on her when you were playing chess."

"She did not speak?"

"You may call her name. She will speak now."

"Kadeejah?"

"Yes, father?"

"Go to your mother," Tyree said, engorged with rage. "You have tried and torn my patience, Kimbene."

"No, I have only shamed you. But I have given you something you could never have, which is voyeurism. Even now you can see me inside her. This is the picture of your rage."

"I will kill you with my bare hands."

"Yes, you think so, but now you are too curious about my second show. You must know what this is, the thing you can never have that I will give you and which will exalt you."

"It can never be enough to erase what you have just done."

"Let's see. Put out your hands and think intently upon that thing that you can never have."

Tyree did so. Then Kimbene bowed before him,

bowed so that his own hair grazed the hands of Tyree.

"You bowed to me," Tyree said. "I saw you bow to me."

"Exactly," Kimbene said.

Tyree was exhilarated, stunned, amazed, and temporarily sighted in his mind. Not only had he seen it happen, but he knew that such a thing should never happen. A regional king had bowed his head to a rural king. He was so transfixed with bliss that he didn't hear Kimbene leave the tent. Nor did Kimbene forget what Tyree had told him. He suspected that the Edo warriors had orders to kill him and Trevor if they tried to leave. And yet when they heard Tyree proclaim loudly from within the tent that he could see, they went running and forgot about Kimbene and Trevor, who left without a single hand raised against them.

"You are marvelous and magical," Trevor said when they were back in the disputed territories again.

"What I did back there would have been enough years ago when I was rural king. But guns have made liars of men and litanies of kings."

"But I heard him," Trevor said. "He said he could see."

"The bristle of hair against hands is enough to make the senses come to life for a moment. No more. Tyree will return to his darkness with a sad longing he has never felt before and a need for vengeance. He will break all bargains."

201

"He doesn't deserve to be called a king."

"There is a disease upon all kingships, Trevor. We have become no more than puppets for stool wives. The old honor is gone."

"Then we have wasted our trip?"

"No. But we must teach both sides with cruelty now."

The next day both Edo and Ibo armies advanced upon the land between them, ready for more war. But Kimbene spoke to the land and it quaked and trembled, opening up for him and swallowing soldiers of both tribes, who fell between the cracks, screamed with horrible voices, and then were heard no more, as the ground came back together again.

"I can't believe what I have witnessed," Trevor said. "How will this be told?"

"Some will call it earthquake," Kimbene said. "Some will say that natural gas exploded. Others will speak of dynamite. But no one will account for all these bodies, which I have buried. You tremble, Trevor?"

"I'm a bit afraid to be near you."

"Do not fear. You will be the only witness. And you have witnessed my last and best show of power."

"You speak as though you're leaving."

"What every man knows, if he knows nothing else, is the way home. The door swings in four directions."

XIX

They had no need of alarm clocks. A cockatoo awoke all the stool wives at dawn's early light, and in various stages of undressing, gradual deshabille, they went to the spacious kitchen, either for eating or cooking or both.

They had all the latest appliances: a frigidaire, a dishwasher, a Dutch-oven toaster, a microwave that nobody understood. Cast iron pans hung on the walls where ebony masks used to hang. Some of the older stool wives, like Stella and Della, still wore traditional dress, while some of the younger ones wore blue jeans and sneakers. Mary, Diana and Florence danced and sang while they worked. Cindi did yoga. Miriam gouged a grapefruit with a serrated spoon. Esther sat apart from the others, rollers in her hair, chewing gum and filing her nails.

Della was teaching Hannah how to make spaghetti for twenty.

"First, you put grease in pan. Then cebollas, leeks or whatever onions. Maybe garlic. Then you sautee your goat strips. Then you stomp tomatoes like cassava and throw them in. Keep the seeds too. Add some water, salt, hot peppers, anything else you got left over."

"Smells good," Hannah said.

"A tally-talker named Caruso taught me this. It's a number one recipe. You never know when you gonna have a war."

"I want some bagels and cream cheese," Esther said.

"Aren't we the hungry ones?" Stella teased her. "Shall I serve you, Es—stair?"

They had all taken to calling her by her French name, accent compliments of Okolo.

"No," Esther said. "I'm watching my weight."

"You can't hurry love," Florence said.

"Stop," Mary said, "in the name of love."

They all twittered. Everyone had had children by Kimbene, except Esther. Stella and Della had sons in America, Mike at UCLA, Moustafa at Notre Dame, both on basketball scholarships. Their daughters Molly and Millie were grown and married to Ibo rural kings. The grounds were swelled with little children, and they all ganged up on the virgin Esther. She had never told anyone of her night of flesh with Kimbene.

"She saves herself," Della said, "by watching her

weight. Would you watch mine, Hannah? I haven't got the temporality."

They all laughed again.

"You are all hens," Esther said. "Our lord deserves better."

"He has no complaints," Stella said. "We are nine and ever ready, like the batteries."

They all laughed again.

"Did you notice he has grown a gray hair or two?" Diana said.

"Not where I'm looking," Florence said.

"How would you rate him, Miriam?" Mary asked. "You've had many entries."

"He is better than most," she said, grapefruit sticking to her teeth. "He doesn't beat me afterwards."

"I was talking technique," Mary added.

"He knows where to look," she said, "and where not to look. This is important. He takes long enough that I can close my eyes and go away, but not so long that I come back and it hurts."

"Does he ever do anything . . . unnatural?" Esther asked.

They all laughed again.

"He always does something unnatural," Della said.

"He quotes Shakespeare when he comes," Cindi said from her asana.

"He tells me my ass could sink a thousand ships," Florence said.

"He sometimes calls me Naomi," Miriam said.

"That's a compliment," Stella told her. "She knew how to make him dance."

"Sometimes," Hannah said, "he speaks of fires and absence and writing, even while we are engaged, and he gets a faraway look and forgets to thrust. I find this very compelling."

"There must be more to life," Esther said, "than spreading your legs for a man."

"It's not the spreading," Stella said. "It's the joy of spreading. You open your legs to a man like that and take him in. For that time you are him. It always swells me."

"Even after all these years?" Esther asked. "Don't you get tired of it?"

"I thought I might," Stella said. "But there have been moons when he stopped coming. And then I thought, 'Fine, it is over now, and you will raise your children.' I felt older and wiser. And then he would look upon me, then take me, and I would feel foolish and younger again. And he never took me just to take me. This is what I treasure: he has never taken me for granted."

"Is that your experience too, Della?" Florence asked.

"Mine is different, but the same. Even when we were little children and I would try to catch his eye, I knew that Stella would be first stool. I used to think, 'How can I look more like Stella?' And then one day he gave me some coral beads. He was so tall and awkward. He looked across the grass savannas as he spoke to me and he said he feared women more than anything else in life. I touched

206

his hand and he ran away. It was then I knew it didn't matter where I sat among his stools."

"A touching story," Esther said. "A poignant narrative. But it lacks a little in later romancing."

"What does romancing have to do with what happens between men and women?" Hannah asked. "I have seen women sold for stones."

"Barleycorn," Mary said.

"A barrel of oil," Florence said.

"I wish he would come around more often," Miriam said.

"Some nights he just plays chess with Trevor in the darkness," Hannah said.

"That's what men do when they get older," Diana said. "They discover the company of other men."

"But what can another man give that we can't?" Mary asked.

"Another manhood," Stella said, looking at Della. "In the same way that we are married more to each other than to him."

"Don't you think," Della said to Stella, "that Trevor begins to look like a black man?"

"The longer he stays, yes."

"Me, I've been looking at Al and Ed," Cindi said. "Sometimes at night I dream I'm a parachute woman and I drop from a cloud onto their steeples."

"What does this mean?" Mary asked.

"Never mind her," Miriam said. "She dropped many acids in the Sixties."

"Any of you ever have a fantasy about Okolo?"

Hannah asked. "He speaks the language of love."

"He's a one-track train," Cindi said. "And no caboose."

"Do women ever talk about anything else but men?" Esther said, still hungry for bagels and cream cheese.

"Children," Stella said.

"Food," Della said.

"Clothing," Florence said.

"Other women," Diana said.

"What do you want to talk about?" Hannah asked.

"Our fathers," Esther said. "Our dreams. Our diaries. Sisterhood. Stuff like that. I mean, are stool wives really necessary?"

"Africa would evaporate without them," Stella said.

"Men like to be myths," Della said. "They dream of nothing else. We are left to be the reality."

"Can you clarify with a metaphor?" Esther asked.

"Of course. Take the newspaper."

"I wish I could," Cindi said. "They don't deliver out here."

"Men are like the print," Della said. "If you rub the print with your finger, it smears. If you rub hard enough, it will even go away. But there is still the paper. Stool wives are the paper. Men are the print, which changes from day to day."

"There is something very profound in what you

say," Esther said, "which clashes with this something very mundane that I feel."

"The distance between those two things is your lifespan," Stella said.

"Can we turn on the television?" Cindi said. "I don't want to miss my programs."

"What are your programs?" Hannah asked.

"FLINTSTONES and HONEYMOONERS."

"They are the same," Florence said.

"Yes," Hannah said. "Sameness attracts me. I began by being bored. I am by now addicted."

"I hate reruns," Diana said.

"I like sequels, myself," Mary said.

"They also are the same," Florence said.

The television was turned on, but only the images. No sound. As though by instinctual cue, many of the stool wives began singing slowly and plaintively the words to the Otis Redding tune, "Sitting on the Dock of the Bay," so slowly that it sounded like a soulful song, a mournful dirge.

Stella and Della stood alone at last at the back door, which looked out upon the picnic tables and the palanquin, the sand box and swing sets, and beyond those the grass savannas.

"Do you think he will come tonight?" Della asked.

Stella squeezed Della's hand. That was her answer.